Job:

Private Investigator's Assistant
Long hours, low pay, hard work.
Based on the Shady Side of town!

Vampire seeks chef

... for lunch

YOUR EYES ARE CLOSED. YOU'RE leaning back in your chair and drifting off when a low gravelly voice disturbs you.

"Hey, I don't pay you to snooze. Look sharp!"

A familiar white furry face looms over you. Two oily black eyes. One wet pink nose. This is Klaus Solstaag: a private investigator, your boss and a yeti.

"I nip out for five minutes and when I get back I find you taking a nap. I know you said you had a bad night's sleep but I need you alert now."

Klaus turns on one of the many fans. The cold breeze makes you sit bolt upright. It catches a pile of newspapers, blowing them around the already messy office.

"We have a visitor," he says.

You've learned a lot about Haventry since Klaus hired you as his assistant. For the most part, it's a quiet, ordinary town, but its shady side is home to every mythical being imaginable – and even a few you never dared to imagine.

The hairs on your arms stand on end as a shadow appears at the frosted windowpane. You never know who or what will walk through that door next.

When it does suddenly swing open, a man in a white lab coat bursts into the room. On his head, he wears a pair of goggles strapped over an explosion of white hair.

"Dr Franklefink," says Klaus.

"Detective Inspector Solstaag," replies the man.

"Actually, it's plain old Mr Solstaag since I quit the Unusual Police Force," says Klaus.

"Sorry, yes. Force of habit," replies the doctor. "It's a good thing you're no longer with the UPF, though. I need someone independent and trustworthy." His eyes swivel round to you. "Who's this?"

"My new assistant," says Klaus.

"What happened to your last one?"

"Ah, poor old Edwin the Elf went in to investigate that bottomless well behind the supermarket and never came out," says Klaus. "I did warn him that you can't get to the bottom of every single mystery."

Klaus chuckles but you wonder whether it's really a joke. How many assistants has he had? How many has he lost?

Dr Franklefink addresses you directly. "It's dangerous, working with this yeti. You should be careful. Hold on, are you ... a human?"

Before you can answer, Klaus says, "Need I remind *you* that you are also human, doctor?"

"Yes, but—"

Klaus interrupts. "Let me assure you that my assistant is both discreet and diligent. Now, please take a seat and tell me what we can do for you."

The doctor hesitates, then reluctantly sits down. "Someone has stolen a very precious object from me," says Dr Franklefink. "It is the most valuable piece of equipment I own – made by my great-great-grandfather. It is called..." The doctor stands up, raises his arms to the ceiling and cries, "The Monster Maker!" Klaus coughs politely and the doctor sits back down.

"Sorry," he says. "Force of habit. But you must return it to me. Since my great-great-grandfather created it, each generation of Franklefinks has used it to weave the purple hair that brings our creations to life."

He pulls out a handful of photographs showing various monsters. The older photos are black and white but those in colour reveal that all the monsters have the same bright purple hair.

"Talk us through what happened," says Klaus. "Let's start with the last time you saw this contraption."

"I saw it yesterday morning when I went into the lab to check that everything was going according to plan."

"Working on a new monster, are you?" asks Klaus.

"Oh yes," says the doctor, eyes wide with excitement. "A beautiful monster, my masterpiece. This one will overshadow all my other creations."

"You've only ever made one," says Klaus. "Talking of which, how is Monty?"

"He's a good boy but he needs a mother. That is why I'm creating..." He pauses for dramatic effect. "Enormelda!"

Klaus laughs and the doctor looks offended.

"Sorry," says Klaus. "I mean... No, it's a lovely name."

"It is and yet she lies lifeless – and *hair*less – on my lab table. I cannot complete the project without the Monster Maker."

Klaus checks that you have your notepad at the ready. He relies on you to jot down all the facts.

He may be a brilliant detective but, as the messy office indicates, his organizational skills are lacking. That's why he needs you.

"When did you realize it was missing?" Klaus asks the doctor.

"Late yesterday afternoon," the doctor replies. "My son had some friends over for a party. After they'd left, I discovered that the Monster Maker was gone."

"What does it look like, this Monster Maker?"

"I have a picture." He shows you one of the monster photos. In the background is a metal object that looks like an old-fashioned sewing machine, covered in cogs and with steam billowing out of the top.

"Is it heavy?" asks Klaus.

"Well, it's obviously light enough for someone to walk off with, otherwise I wouldn't be here, would I?" replies the doctor irritably.

Klaus winks at you. The doctor may not like all these questions but you both know how important every detail can be in a case like this.

"Talk us through the day," says Klaus.

"Very well." The doctor sighs. "After I left the lab, I went to find Monty. I called for him but, before I could locate him, there was a knock at the door. It was Witches' Oven, the catering company. It's run by two witches, Burnella and Bridget Milkbird. The food isn't great, but they're cheap."

"Hm, I know those two," says Klaus. "They've both stirred up trouble over the years."

"I don't think they had anything to do with it," says the doctor. "All they stir up is inedible food."

"Rule number one," says Klaus. "No one is above suspicion."

Your boss gives Dr Franklefink a long hard stare. It's clear to you that he's implying even the doctor himself should be on your list of suspects, but Dr Franklefink shrugs it off. "I just don't want you to waste your time talking to them."

"Even if they didn't take it, they might have seen something," says Klaus. "So what happened next?"

"I showed the witches to the kitchen, then heard another knock at the door. This time it was the entertainer I booked for the party, Deadzo the zombie clown."

"He sounds like a barrel of laughs," replies Klaus.

"I usually use the illusionist The Great Impossible, but Monty said he wanted something different this year, as he's nine now. Making balloon animals that run around the room is all well and good but I think that nine-year-olds require more sophisticated entertainment."

"Such as a zombie clown?" Klaus looks amused.

"Precisely. Although I got the impression he thought it was all a bit beneath him. Anyway, I showed Deadzo to the party room, then went to find Monty. He was outside trying the new bike I'd given him. I'd added rocket boosters to it! I didn't really want him to go for a ride until I'd tightened his stitches, though. Monty's very delicate. I don't allow him to go to the hairdressers in case they nip a stitch and unravel him. I was young when I made him…"

"I see. But his stitching was OK, was it?" asks Klaus.

"Oh yes, a couple of them were coming loose around the right ear but nothing much."

"Tell me about the party," says Klaus.

"What's to say? Monty's friends arrived, Deadzo did his thing, everyone had a good time, the food came out, followed by the cake. Then, once everyone had gone home, I went back to the lab and discovered that the Monster Maker was gone."

"How many friends were there?"

"Five. There was Lana. She's a ghost. I wouldn't waste much time on her. I'm not even sure she can pick up things and besides, she's pretty transparent. I mean, you can literally see through her."

The doctor sniggers at his joke but Klaus is concentrating. "Do carry on," he urges.

"Monty invited the goblin twins Grundle and Grinola Squelch as well," says Dr Franklefink. "They were dropped off by their grandma, Ma Squelch. However, it turned out that they're allergic to milk so they reacted rather badly to the cake. This morning I had to have my whole house professionally cleaned!"

"Goblins and trouble go together like cold days and hot chocolate," Klaus explains to you.

"And then there was Trisha Cry's lad, Huey."

"They're werewolves," Klaus informs you.

"But your prime suspects should be the Stokers," says Dr Franklefink. "Bobby is Monty's best friend, but it's his bloodsucking father, Bramwell, who I really don't trust. Yes, that vampire is by far the most likely culprit."

"If you're so sure, why do you need me?" asks Klaus. "And, while we're at it, why didn't you call the Unusual Police Force?"

"I need you to find the proof that reveals Bramwell Stoker is the thief." Dr Franklefink gets up to leave but then he pauses at the door. "The UPF are all very well and good, but they can be rather slow and I need results quickly. You can find me at City Chamber tonight – brings your findings to me there."

Once the doctor has gone, Klaus turns to you. There's a sparkle of excitement in his eyes at the prospect of a mystery to solve. You can't help smiling.

He says, "OK, so you should have a list of everyone who visited the house, including the parents and guardians who dropped off the kids."

You look at your list to check that you haven't missed anyone, then Klaus says, "Come on. We'll take the dog."

You grab your coat and follow Klaus through the door, down the stairs, out into the street, where his car is parked.

Klaus's car, Watson, is a brown, flaky rust-bucket covered in dents and scratches, but Klaus has great affection for it, not least because Watson used to be his pet dog.

When you first started working for Klaus, he explained that Watson had been the best detective dog he'd ever owned until a witch called Susan turned him into a car. The spell bounced off his wing mirror and transformed her into a caravan, meaning he was stuck like this.

Klaus pats Watson's bonnet and says, "Who's a good car? You're a good car. Yes, you are." He slips into the driver's seat and you get in next to him. "So where are we taking him first?" he asks.

? Do you want to start working through the list of suspects?
Turn to page 21
THE WEREWOLF & THE VAMPIRE

? Or do you want to investigate the crime scene?
Turn to page 31
THE MAD SCIENTIST'S LAB

THE WEREWOLF & THE VAMPIRE

"IT MAKES SENSE TO START with Huey Cry and his mum as they're the furthest away," says Klaus. "Their house is in the borough of West Leafington over in the human part of town. Everyone else lives here on the Shady Side."

Sitting on Watson's furry seats, you feel your elbow itch. You're pretty sure Watson has fleas but you don't complain. He may be a bit smelly but he's loyal and he often turns up exactly where you need him, even if he does have a habit of leaving oil puddles at the bottom of trees.

The quiet suburb where the Crys live is a contrast to the Shady Side where Klaus's office is based.

The neighbours' curtains twitch as you stride up the driveway. They probably think Klaus is a large man in a fur coat. In this part of town no one would expect to see a yeti any more than they would consider the possibility that their neighbours are werewolves.

You arrive at Trisha Cry's house. There are hanging baskets outside, brimming with brightly coloured flowers.

"The thing about werewolves is that most of the time they can pass themselves off as regular folk," says Klaus. "It's only once a month they get ... you know ... howly and bitey."

Your nerves are jangling like the wind chime that hangs outside the front door. You're about to meet a real-life werewolf. If that isn't scary enough, there's a full moon tonight. You almost jump out of your skin when the door opens.

Trisha Cry has her wavy brown hair up in a ponytail and wears a pair of yellow washing-up gloves on her hands. From the kitchen you can smell steak sizzling and hear the sound of the radio.

"Mr Solstaag," she says, "please come in. Don't stay there on the doorstep drawing attention to yourself."

She ushers you both inside.

"What can I do for you?" She hurriedly closes the door behind you.

"We'd like to have a word with you and your son," he replies.

"Huey's not here. He's taken the bus to school." Mrs Cry sighs. "But tell me, what's he done now?"

That's an interesting response. Klaus raises an eyebrow and says, "It's in connection with a stolen item."

Mrs Cry nods sadly. "Oh dear. Huey has a problem. We're working through it. He's a good boy at heart but the wolf in him makes him a little..."

She pauses, so Klaus prompts her. "Are you saying he's stolen things before?"

"Well, mostly chickens, but yes, he has stolen before."

It's strange to imagine that once a month this mild-mannered woman turns into a wild animal. The living room you're standing in couldn't be more ordinary if it tried – and you get the feeling it's trying very hard. The cream walls are decorated with pictures of Huey at various ages. Porcelain ornaments adorn the shelves, although the presence of a cardboard box filled with newspaper shows that they are in the process of being packed away. Mrs Cry picks one up and places it in the box.

"We'll be going out this evening but I always prefer to be overcautious," she says by way of explanation. For a moment, you catch a glimpse of the wolf lurking inside as her eyes shine and her nose twitches. "So what's gone missing, anyway?"

"Dr Franklefink's Monster Maker," says Klaus. "It was taken during yesterday's party."

"Oh, in which case it can't have been Huey." She looks relieved.

"You seem very sure."

"I'm positive." There is fresh resolve in Mrs Cry's response. "I picked him up from the party. He was carrying a party bag but nothing else. He certainly didn't have that contraption of Franklefink's."

"It sounds like you know what the Monster Maker looks like."

"I have seen it before, yes," she admits. "Franklefink and I are both on the Board of Governors at the school. I can tell you for certain that my son did not remove the Monster Maker from his house."

You're busily making notes, drawing connections and jotting down possible clues while your boss takes care of the interview.

"OK. One last question," says Klaus. "What were *you* doing during the party?"

"I went to the butcher's," she replies. "At this time of the month, it's best my son and I don't leave the house on an empty stomach." She makes it sound so innocent. "Now, I think I've answered all your questions. It couldn't have been my son and it certainly wasn't me who stole the Monster Maker. Good luck with your investigation."

Next, you visit the Stokers. Their house couldn't be more different from the Crys' suburban home. Right in the heart of the Shady Side of Haventry, they live in a spooky old three-storey building with gargoyles, crooked chimneys and turrets.

Watson comes to a standstill outside and you nervously get out. A chill wind cuts through your clothes. An ominous dark cloud is hanging above the Stokers' house, heavy with the promise of rain.

The gravel crunches beneath your feet and a solitary bat flies out of a hole in the roof. It makes your boss jump.

"I don't like bats," he says. "They're so ... flappy."

It amuses you to think your boss might be scared of something so harmless. It's the vampires that worry you.

When you reach the door, Klaus pulls on a large chain and a distant bell chimes. You wait. Something creaks. You hear the sound of wood against wood. You imagine a coffin lid rising up, then clattering to the ground. You almost jump out of your skin when a pale hand opens the door.

"Oh, hi, Mr Solstaag, sir," says a boy with slick black hair.

"Bobby," says Klaus. "Is your dad in?"

"He has a big debate at City Chamber tonight so he's still sleeping." He sniffs and glances at you. "Which is probably best since you've brought a human with you."

"This one's not on the menu," says Klaus.

You're glad that he's there to protect you.

The sun briefly appears from behind a cloud and Bobby steps back into the hallway, shying away from the light. You spot a selection of umbrellas and hooded cloaks hanging from the coat stand just inside the door. The vampires use them to move around the city during daylight hours.

"Perhaps we could come in and ask you a few questions," suggests Klaus.

"I suppose..." says Bobby. "What are you investigating?"

"Something was stolen from Dr Franklefink's lab yesterday."

"Really?" says Bobby. "Who are your suspects?"

"We're whittling down our list at the moment," replies Klaus.

It's gloomy inside the house. Flickering candlelight illuminates patterned wallpaper that seems to shift when you're not looking directly

at it; you feel as though you're being watched. You try to control your fear as you take out your notepad. You're glad that Klaus stays on the doorstep.

"Did you go into the lab yesterday?" asks Klaus.

"No," replies Bobby. "The last time I went in, Dr Franklefink got really angry with me for knocking over a jar of molars. I told him not to cry over spilled milk teeth but that didn't seem to help."

"Funny," says Klaus, although there's no trace of a smile on his face. He remains focused. "So you've been in the lab before. Did you see anybody go in there during the party?"

"Anyone could have," says Bobby. "We played hide-and-seek."

"Who was the seeker?" asks Klaus.

"Huey. Honestly, I don't even know why Monty invited him. He's so … ordinary. He creeps everyone out."

"In my experience there's no such thing as ordinary. Whether you're from the Shady Side or not, we're all unusual enough to be interesting." Klaus winks at you.

You don't react. You're trying to remain calm and professional but when you're interviewing a vampire that isn't easy. The house is alive with squeaks and

creaks, and you haven't forgotten that a much older –
and deadlier – vampire is sleeping downstairs.

"Anyway, so I hid under Monty's bed," said Bobby.
"It's a pretty good hiding space and I should have won."

"Who did win?" asks Klaus.

"Grundle and Grinola, but I think they cheated."

"How can you cheat at hide-and-seek?"

"If anyone can find a way, it would be those
goblins. They're always up to something. I bet they
were the ones who took the doctor's Monster Maker."

Klaus pauses and glances at you. "Did I mention
it was the Monster Maker that had
gone missing?"

You're pretty sure he didn't.

"Didn't you?" says Bobby.

"No," says Klaus.

"Now I think about it …
Monty must have mentioned
it when he called last night."

"Why did Monty call?"
Klaus's nostrils flare. You've seen
him do this before. It means he's
found a thread worth pulling.

"We're best friends – we talk all
the time! Maybe you should ask

him what happened yesterday. It was his party after all." Bobby's noticed the change in Klaus's tone too. He shifts uncomfortably and looks at his watch. "I'm sorry. I need to get ready for school. I don't want to be late. Good luck finding the machine."

You step back and he slams the door behind you.

"Interesting," says Klaus. "He's definitely hiding something. In my experience, vampires aren't the most trustworthy folk in the Shady Side."

You're just pleased to be walking away from the house. You realize you've been clenching your fists. There are white marks where you've dug your nails into the palms.

Your yeti boss turns to you and says, "So, where should our investigation take us next?"

You respond:

? "Let's go and talk to the goblins."
Turn to page 54
MA SQUELCH

? "I think we need to speak to Monty."
Turn to page 31
THE MAD SCIENTIST'S LAB

THE MAD SCIENTIST'S LAB

KLAUS DRIVES WATSON IN THE direction of Dr Franklefink's house but stops on the way to visit a sandwich bar called Hob-Gobbling.

When you come out, Watson has gone.

"This is one of the problems with driving a car that is actually a bewitched dog," says Klaus. "He's probably off chasing other cars. He likes to sniff their exhaust pipes. We'll have to walk."

Klaus wolfs down a baguette as long as your arm on the way. Your boss has a big appetite. When you're on an investigation you usually carry a chocolate bar for him in your pocket. He gets grouchy when he's hungry and he thinks more clearly on a full stomach.

When you arrive at the doctor's house, Klaus knocks on the door.

The boy who answers has large stitches across his forehead, down his neck and round his wrists. You understand what Dr Franklefink means about Monty not being his best work. His grey skin is rather flappy in places, one ear is higher than the other and the mop of fuzzy purple hair on his head clashes horribly with his green school jumper.

"Ah, Monty, is it me or have you grown?" asks Klaus, sounding a bit like a kindly uncle. Sometimes it seems as though your boss knows everyone on this side of town, probably from his stint working for the Unusual Police Force.

"It must be you," replies the boy miserably. "The only way I can grow is if Dad makes me some longer limbs and he says he hasn't the parts for that at the moment."

"And I guess they would cost an arm and a leg," chuckles Klaus.

"It's not the money," says Monty with a sorrowful nod. "He just can't be bothered." He wipes his eye and you notice a stitch above his left eyebrow coming loose.

"Did you have a good birthday?" asks Klaus.

"The party was fun. The zombie clown was a bit weird, but I enjoyed the game of hide-and-seek, even if I was the first to be found. But then, after all my friends had gone, Dad ruined it when he started going on about his stupid Monster Maker. He cares more about *making* monsters than actually looking after the ones he's already made."

"Do you have any idea who took it?" asks Klaus.

"Well, it wasn't me, if that's what you're suggesting," says Monty defensively.

"No one's accusing anyone yet," says Klaus calmly.

"As I said to Bobby on the phone yesterday, anyone could have taken it," continues Monty.

"You and Bobby are pretty good friends, are you?" says Klaus.

"Yes," says Monty glumly, "but Dad doesn't like me going round to his house so we talk a lot on the phone."

"Why wouldn't he want you going to your best friend's house?"

"He doesn't get on with Bobby's dad."

"Yes, I got that impression when he came to the office," says Klaus. "Is your father in now?"

"No. Sorry."

"We'd like to take a look around if that's OK."

"I suppose that would be all right," says Monty.

You follow him into the hall, then down the spiral staircase to a windowless room that screams *mad scientist's lab* thanks to the bubbling test tubes, hissing petri dishes and pulsating body parts in jars. In the centre of the lab, covered in a red cloth, is a lifeless body, the size of a large adult and totally bald.

"I'm guessing this must be Dr Franklefink's latest project, Enormelda," says Klaus.

The whole place is a health-and-safety nightmare, with razor-sharp scalpels on the lab tables and noxious fumes wafting around. You're careful not

to touch anything as you follow Monty to the shelf where the Monster Maker was kept. You take a closer look and spot the dusty outline where the object stood. On the floor beneath it are a few small brown pellets.

Klaus drops to his knees, picks one up and sniffs it. "Hmm, do you have a rodent problem?"

"One of the lab mice probably escaped again," says Monty.

"Do you have a cleaner?" asks Klaus.

"Dad had to get those cleaning unicorns in after the goblins puked at my party but he wouldn't usually allow anyone in the lab."

"Not even you?"

"Why would I want to come in here?" says Monty, shoving his hands into his pockets.

"You're not interested in your father's work?" enquires Klaus.

"I *am* my father's work," Monty replies. "I don't know why you're asking *me* all these questions. If you want to find Dad's precious device, you should be talking to the suspects."

"And who would you say is most likely?"

You've seen Klaus use this technique before, asking his suspects to point the finger. It doesn't always uncover the guilty party, but you can find out a lot about a suspect from learning who they think committed the crime.

"I don't know," says Monty. "Maybe the goblins. They're always stealing stuff."

You hear the front door slam. "That must be Dad," says Monty. "He won't like you being down here."

You take one last quick look around the lab and try to remember all the details before following Monty back up the staircase.

Dr Franklefink is standing in the hallway.

"What are you doing here?" the doctor demands.

"We've been examining the scene of the crime," says Klaus.

"And? Have you found anything yet?"

Your boss's eyes flash with anger, but he takes a moment and replies in measured tones. "I don't find it helpful to discuss cases while they are ongoing."

"I hired you to find the culprit."

"And I will," says Klaus.

"I hope that at the very least you noticed the bat droppings."

"I did spot something along those lines."

"Where there are bat droppings, there are bats, and where there are bats, there are vampires," states Dr Franklefink.

"If you're so sure of who the thief is, why do you need us?" asks Klaus.

"I need the proof that will bring Stoker to justice and I want the machine returned to me. I shall be attending meetings at the City Chamber this evening – I expect you to report to me there with your findings."

He holds the door open.

"Let's hope we have everything wrapped up by then," says Klaus.

"You'd better," says Dr Franklefink. "Then the whole town will see that vampire for what he is."

"Perhaps," says Klaus. "But we've plenty more suspects to talk to before we draw any conclusions. Good day, doctor."

"Good day to you," says Franklefink.

You follow your boss out on to the pavement

where Watson is waiting for you by the curb, wagging his exhaust pipe and panting.

In the car, Klaus turns to you and says, "If you ask me, Dr Franklefink hasn't told us everything he knows – or possibly he's making out he knows more than he does. Either way, I don't trust him. What do you say we follow him?"

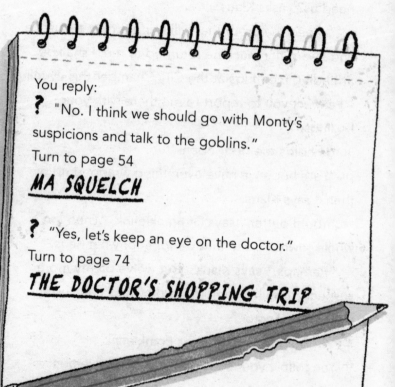

You reply:
? "No. I think we should go with Monty's suspicions and talk to the goblins."
Turn to page 54
MA SQUELCH

? "Yes, let's keep an eye on the doctor."
Turn to page 74
THE DOCTOR'S SHOPPING TRIP

HAVENTRY SCHOOL FOR THE UNUSUALLY GIFTED

YOU'VE OFTEN WONDERED WHAT HAVENTRY School for the Unusually Gifted is like. The receptionist buzzes you in and you wait to be seen. In one sense, the school reception is no different to any primary school in Haventry. There are examples of pupils' work on the wall, photos of the teachers with their names underneath and a noticeboard with announcements about upcoming events.

On the other hand, there's a furious pixie shouting at a receptionist, who looks like she's been dead for at least a couple of years. It takes you a moment to realize that the pixie is a parent rather than a pupil. Once he's finished complaining about his son not making the school basketball team, it's your turn to see the receptionist.

"We're here to talk to some of your pupils," says Klaus.

The receptionist eyes your boss suspiciously, then turns her attention to you. "Oh, are you part of Human Awareness Week? Is it a costume?"

"Yes, we're doing an assembly," lies Klaus.

"It's very realistic," says the receptionist, examining you. "You can go through and wait in the staffroom."

Klaus is still chuckling about this when a girl carrying a large pile of books collides with you in the corridor. The books tumble to the ground but the girl goes straight through you. You're overcome with a feeling of sadness and self-pity as the spirit travels through your flesh and bones. The next moment, the feeling vanishes.

"I'm so sorry," says the ghost girl. "I wasn't looking where I was going."

You're too shaken by the experience to reply.

One of the books has fallen open on the first page. The girl's name is written inside in pencil.

"Lana," says Klaus. "We have a couple of questions about the party you attended yesterday."

She flings out her arms and bursts into tears with such dramatic flair that, for a moment, you think she's pretending. "I only went to that party because I thought there was going to be ectoplasm jelly," she wails. "Birthday parties make me want to cry."

"What's wrong with birthday parties?" asks Klaus.

"I... I..." She sobs. "I fell asleep on my birthday."

"That doesn't sound so bad," says Klaus.

She stiffens and scowls at Klaus. "I mean, I passed away... You know, I shuffled off this..."

"Oh, I see. You died on your birthday," says Klaus.

"Must you put it so bluntly?" Lana pouts and turns a slow, joyless somersault.

"Sorry, but you are a ghos—"

"Don't say it!" Lana floats up to his level and holds her hands out in an attempt to silence him.

Klaus looks amused but he stifles his smile. "Are you and Monty close friends?"

"Not really, but me and the Franklefinks go way back," replies Lana, a dark look clouding her eyes. "I knew Monty's dad when he was Monty's age. And his grandad. And his great-grandad. And—"

Klaus cuts her off. "And how was the birthday party?"

"It was all right," Lana admits. "I liked it when we played hide-and-seek. I'm good at it! It's one of the few advantages of my condition." She sighs.

"May I ask where you hid?"

"In the walls," she says dreamily. "I like walls – they're cosy."

"The walls of Dr Franklefink's lab, by any chance?" enquires Klaus.

"Oh no, not there. That's where his family creates those horrible monsters."

"Such as your friend Monty," Klaus points out.

"Oh, Monty's all right," replies Lana. "It's not his fault. It's never the children's fault, is it?"

"What isn't?" asks Klaus, intrigued, his nostrils twitching.

"Things," she replies wistfully. "Things are never children's fault, in my experience."

You wonder if there's more to this answer than she's letting on. Certainly, someone who has the ability to hide in walls is likely to see more than most.

"Did you see anything strange at the party?" he asks. "Anything out of the ordinary?"

"Everything's out of the ordinary around here." She drifts down so that she's level with you. "Well, almost everything," she adds, peering into your eyes. You wonder if she experienced your emotions in the same way as you felt hers when she passed through you.

"I mean like someone walking out of Dr Franklefink's lab carrying his Monster Maker," says Klaus.

"I don't know what that is," she replies. She sounds as though she's telling the truth, but as she's transparent it can be hard to read her expressions.

"It's a device for bringing things to life. It looks a bit like a sewing machine with cogs. It's about this big." Klaus demonstrates the size of the Monster Maker. "And it's gone missing."

"Oh," says Lana listlessly. "That explains all the shouting after the party."

43

"So you didn't go home when everyone else did?" asks Klaus.

"No… I lingered." Lana drifts around in a loop. "Unlike the others, I don't have a home to go to. I don't have a family to pick me up. It's no life being a ghost!" She bursts into tears again.

Klaus hands her a tissue from his pocket. She takes it, blows her nose on it and holds it out, dripping in ghostly snot. It occurs to you that if she can hold a tissue and carry books, maybe she would be able to make off with the Monster Maker, but when she tries to put the tissue in her pocket it falls to the ground.

You wonder how it all works. Since taking a job on the Shady Side of town, you've encountered a lot that you don't understand.

"So, you were there when Franklefink discovered it was gone?" says Klaus.

"Yes. I heard him cry out, so I went to see what was wrong. He was yelling about it being an outrage and a plot to bring about his downfall."

"Maybe the Monster Maker could bring you back to life?" suggests Klaus.

"I don't have a body to bring to life," says Lana. "Now, I have to go. I'm supposed to be on prefect duty in the playground."

With that, she's gone, vanishing into a wall as though she was never there at all.

You're about to suggest heading to the staffroom when Klaus raises a large hairy finger to his lips. "Listen," he whispers.

His ears have pricked up. He removes his hat and sniffs as if he's scented something, then creeps up to a locker and in one swift movement, pulls it open. Two small green goblins tumble out.

"Grundle and Grinola Squelch," says your boss. "Why were you spying on us?"

"We weren't spying," replies Grundle. "We were looking for something."

"Something like a Monster Maker, stolen from Dr Franklefink's laboratory?" asks Klaus.

"We don't know nothing about no Monster Maker," says Grinola, sounding very much like she's reading the words.

You notice that the words are indeed written on her hand. You can't tell if your boss has noticed but you suspect he has.

"That's a triple negative," Klaus says. "And I also think it's a lie."

"It ain't no lie!" says Grundle.

"And that's a double negative," replies Klaus.

"So we're heading in the right direction. Now, tell me what you know."

"We don't know nothing about no Monster Maker," says Grinola, once again reading the words from her hand.

"You know it would be better to tell the truth if you are involved, don't you?" says Klaus.

"Tell what tooth?" says Grundle.

"He said truth not tooth," says Grinola. "You can't tell teeth anything."

"You can lie through them, though," quips Klaus.

"Yeah, well. We don't know nothing about no Monster Maker," says Grinola for a third time.

"And definitely no one told us to say that," says Grundle.

"Ah." Klaus leans forwards so that his fur tickles the goblins. "So no one told you to say nothing. And did the same no one who didn't tell you to say nothing also write that on your sister's hand?"

"I wrote it on my own hand," says Grinola, although she doesn't look especially convinced by what she's saying.

"I just want to know who you aren't trying to protect. Who doesn't want you to talk about the Monster Maker?"

"Huey," says Grundle at the same time as Grinola says, "Bobby Stoker."

"Both of them?" says Klaus.

The goblins turn to each other.

"Grundle," says Grinola.

"Grinola," says Grundle.

"Tell me what you know," demands Klaus.

"Neither of us knows nothing," says Grundle. "Listen, you can't just come into our school and start questioning us. I demand to see a lawyer."

"Do you know what a lawyer is?" asks Klaus.

"Ma Squelch says it's a thing you need when you is in trouble for doing something," says Grundle.

"Or *not* doing it," adds Grinola. "Because we don't know nothing about no Monster Maker."

The goblins tumble off down the corridor, barging into a group of fairies and causing havoc.

Klaus turns to you. "It'll be break time shortly. I think we should hang around and see who else we can talk to. What do you say?"

? You agree with him.
Turn to page 49

LONE WEREWOLF

? You have had enough of the school and want to go after the witches.
Turn to page 66

THE WITCHES' OVEN

LONE WEREWOLF

A BELL TOLLS FROM A high tower and the pupils of Haventry School for the Unusually Gifted spill out into the playground. You spot Monty and Bobby by the bins, deep in conversation. Grundle and Grinola swing from the monkey bars, fighting, shouting and tumbling. You can't see Lana the ghost but you do spot Huey Cry, sitting on a bench under a willow tree. As you approach, he looks up at you sullenly.

"I thought you'd come looking for me eventually," he says.

"Why did you think that?" asks Klaus.

"Because Monty told me about the Monster Maker going missing and I always get blamed for stuff like that.

Just because I stole a couple of chickens. What do people expect? I'm a werewolf."

"I'm not interested in blame," says Klaus. "I've been employed to find something that has gone missing. All I want to know is if you can help me find it."

"It wasn't me who took it from the lab."

Klaus snorts and nudges you. "How do you know it was stolen?"

Huey scratches his head. You take a small step back, wondering whether werewolves are as susceptible to fleas as dogs.

"It could have been mislaid," continues Klaus. "It could have just vanished into thin air. When you're investigating something on the Shady Side, anything is possible."

"Still seems most likely it's been stolen, if you ask me." Huey shrugs.

"So who do you think stole it, then?"

"I don't know. I didn't see anything and it's nothing to do with me."

Huey stares defiantly at the huge, lumbering mountain of white fur that is your boss.

"Don't you think the thief should be caught?" asks Klaus.

"Why should I care?"

"Because Monty is your friend, isn't he?"

"Not really. His dad forced him to invite me to the party. They all steer clear of me…" He sniffs sadly.

"Why do you think that?" asks Klaus.

"I'm too ordinary," says Huey miserably. "That's the problem with being a werewolf. This school is for the *unusually gifted*. I haven't got any gifts and for twenty-nine or thirty days of the month, there's nothing unusual about me either. I can't walk through walls. I can't breathe fire or fly, or turn into a cat, or gnaw through metal. I can't do anything. Then, when there's a full moon, I turn into a wild animal. The only time I *do* fit in, I'm not allowed near anyone." Huey bursts into tears and lets out a bloodcurdling howl.

You feel sorry for him but you stay quiet.

"You aren't alone in feeling like a misfit." Klaus glances at you. "We all do sometimes."

"Yeah, well…" Huey kicks a pebble and thrusts his hands into his pockets.

"Lana mentioned a game of hide-and-seek," says Klaus.

"Yes, I was seeking," says Huey. "I sniffed them all out pretty quickly. Except Lana, of course. She's impossible to find."

"In what order did you find them?"

"Er, I think it was the goblins, Monty then Bobby. No, sorry. That can't be right because the goblins won. They must have been last."

"What about Lana?"

"We let her play but we don't count her because she never gets found. Sometimes I wish I was a ghost. At least I'd be good at something then."

"Did you bump into anyone else while you were looking for the others?" asks Klaus.

"I think I saw one of those witches wandering around upstairs," replies Huey.

"Burnella or Bridget?" says Klaus.

"Yes."

"Which?"

"Yes, a witch," says Huey. "They creep me out.

I heard they turned the school caretaker into a dung beetle."

Out of the corner of your eye you notice a six-foot-tall dung beetle jangling a large set of keys and telling a group of children to stop climbing the school walls, until a dragon flies overhead and spits out a mouthful of fire.

"That's the end of break," says Huey.

"In which case, thanks for your time," replies Klaus before turning to you. "Come on, let's get going."

Back inside the car, you flick through your notes, trying to decide what to do next. Your boss is waiting for you to speak, but what should you say?

You reply:
? "We should talk to the witches."

Turn to page 66
THE WITCHES' OVEN

? "Let's get back to the office and do a little research."

Turn to page 86
A LITTLE RESEARCH

MA SQUELCH

"FOR CENTURIES, GOBLINS LIVED IN caves deep underground, only surfacing to cause mischief and mayhem," Klaus explains as you follow him down the subway steps. "And to be honest, nothing's changed."

At the bottom of the steps is a sign that reads: *PRIVATE. NO ENTRY!* Klaus knocks on the door.

The subway smells like an ogre's toilet. You hold your breath while you wait.

"I know this is your first encounter with these goblins but I've had to ask Ma Squelch questions in connection with a number of crimes over the years," he says. "She's committed a fair few but she's also helped me solve some too. She isn't all bad but I'd keep your wits about you. Oh, and keep hold of your pencil and pad. They can be a bit light-fingered, these goblins."

There's a click and a creak followed by the appearance of a tiny goblin. He looks up at Klaus, then screams, "MA SQUELCH!"

Klaus stoops and steps inside. The entrance hall is decorated with garish green wallpaper. Goblin children, goblin toddlers and goblin babies spill out into the hallway, chattering, laughing, gurgling and spitting. You try to avoid treading on any of them as you take a few cautious steps inside.

"Visitors," says a craggy-faced adult goblin wearing an apron that reads: *Goblin all the cakes since 1258*. Her teeth look as though they have all gone rotten, fallen out, then been shoved back into her gums. "If I'd known we were having visitors I'd have tidied up."

She picks up a tin cup and lobs it over her head. It clatters to the ground out of sight. "That's better," she says.

"Ma Squelch. It's been a while," says Klaus, as if he were greeting an old work colleague.

"Not quite long enough, though," she replies, but she actually seems quite pleased to see him. "What can I do you for, Solstaag?"

Everywhere you look, there are young goblins: sitting on chairs eating bowls of spaghetti worms, or skidding around the kitchen floor, crashing into bins. Her grand-goblins are hanging from light fittings, climbing on furniture, kicking things over and walloping each other.

Ma Squelch grabs a tin spoon and bangs it on a saucepan, creating a loud *CLANG! CLANG! CLANNNG!* that silences the other goblins.

"We're here to see Grundle and Grinola," says Klaus. "It's about a theft from Dr Franklefink's lab."

Ma Squelch's eyes narrow. "Don't you go accusing my grand-gobbles. As soon as anything goes missing, us goblin folk are the first to be blamed! Missing cake, missing television, missing baby. It's always our fault."

"Yes, but in those cases, it *was* you." Klaus grins.

"Yeah, well, it ain't us this time. Who's this then? New dogsbody, Klaus?" Ma Squelch jabs a stubby green finger into your chest.

"Leave my assistant alone," says Klaus. "If we could just have a word with the children?"

"You're too late," snaps Ma Squelch. "They're at school."

"Am I correct in thinking that you dropped them off and picked them up from Monty's birthday party yesterday in your goblin truck?" asks Klaus.

"Now you're accusing me, are you? The cheek of it!" squawks Ma Squelch.

"No one is accusing anyone," says Klaus calmly. "I'm just trying to establish a sequence of events."

"A what of what?"

"I need to know what happened when," Klaus clarifies. "If they're as innocent as you suggest, then it's in your best interests to tell me the truth."

"The truth." Ma Squelch sniffs. "Here's the truth. I dropped off my grand-gobbles at Franklefink's house. When I picked them up they were throwing up like there was no tomorrow. It was raining carrots and dogs, I tell you."

Klaus wrinkles his nose, clearly as revolted by this conversation as you are.

"Did they have anything on them?"

"Yes, I just told you. They had sick all over them."

"I imagine it would be easy for Grundle and Grinola to walk out with the Monster Maker in all that chaos."

You're trying to concentrate on your notes but you begin to feel a little queasy yourself.

"All I know is that I brought them home, put them to bed, then set about the van with a mop. I had to throw it away afterwards. I should charge old Franklefink for it. It was him what made them sick in the first place with that cake. I told that man they had allergies, but did he listen? No. Humans never listen – no offence." She adds this looking at you.

"It doesn't sound like you're much of a Franklefink

fan," says Klaus.

"He's an awful man. I wouldn't trust him as far as I could throw him. I wouldn't even trust him as far as I can throw Gronger here."

She picks up one of the children by the armpits.

"Gerroff me," complains the goblin.

Realizing she can't throw him at all, Ma Squelch drops the child. He lands on her toe, causing her to scream at the top of her voice.

Klaus persists. "You didn't see anything suspicious? For example, any of the other children or parents carrying something that could have been the Monster Maker."

"Nope. Chances are, Franklefink made the whole thing up. Now, if you don't mind, you and your pet human –" she looks at you again – "can clear off out of my home."

"OK. We'll go," says Klaus, "but I still want to ask Grundle and Grinola a couple of questions."

"If you know what's good for you, you'll leave me and my grand-gobbles out of this." She shoos you out.

"It's been a pleasure as always," says Klaus.

As grouchy as Ma Squelch's words may have sounded, you sense real affection between your boss and this suspect. Once you're outside, away from the goblins, Klaus turns to face you.

"Like I said, I've known Ma Squelch a long time. When you spend that long working with someone, even when you're on opposite sides of the law, you can end up getting on. I thought she was telling the truth but it's your call."

You're still clutching your notepad. You've made some notes, although something green and sludgy has spilled on them. You don't want to think about what it might be. Your boss is looking at you expectantly. He's waiting for you to decide what should be next in your investigation.

? Do you want to look for Grundle and Grinola at school?

Turn to page 39

HAVENTRY SCHOOL FOR THE UNUSUALLY GIFTED

? Or do you think your time would be better spent following Dr Franklefink?

Turn to page 74

THE DOCTOR'S SHOPPING TRIP

THE NIGHT MAYOR

YOU'RE BACK IN WATSON'S PASSENGER seat and you've just told your boss what you witnessed in the car park.

"Interesting." Klaus strokes his chin as he listens. "I'm glad you told me … except for the bit about the bats. I really don't like bats." He shudders. "When we first spoke to Dr Franklefink, he made it clear that he thinks Bramwell stole the Monster Maker, but you should always be cautious if you feel like you're being drawn to look in one direction. It usually means you should look the other way."

You're still mulling this over as Klaus continues.

"The question is whether Franklefink knew you were there, watching him in the car park. He could well be trying to manipulate our investigation. Whatever he's up to, he's still on my list of likely liars, but the fact that Stoker is running for Night Mayor could well be relevant too. It's a pretty important position in this town. I think we need to talk to our vampire friend to get his side of things."

This is what you love about the job: piecing the clues together, discovering which threads are worth pulling and which will lead you astray. Every witness you speak to gives you a different view of what happened. You have to find the truth at the heart of this web of possibilities.

The plan is to go to Bramwell Stoker's house but you find him before that. He's driving around the Shady Side of Haventry in a long black car with a picture of his face on the top and the words:

VOTE FOR STOKER!
YOU CAN COUNT ON ME

A voice blares out of the loudspeaker on the roof: "Vote for Bramwell Stoker as Haventry's next Night Mayor. A vote for me is a vote for experience. It is a vote for your *future*. I pledge to *sink my teeth* into the issues and to *drain this town of crime*."

Klaus pulls alongside the car at a set of lights. Someone has graffitied a big arrow pointing to Stoker's head and the words:

NEVER TRUST A BALDY

"That's the thing about the Shady Side," explains Klaus. "A lot of us are pretty hairy. Werewolves, bugbears, minotaurs, yetis... All hairy. Goblins, pixies and elves have enough ear hair to stuff a cushion! Wizards tend to favour the bearded look and most witches look like they've never seen the inside of a hairdresser's. We find it hard to trust anyone bald."

Klaus stops Watson in the right-hand lane and you spot Bramwell Stoker in the front of the car. He leans out of the window and says, "Ah, Klaus Solstaag. I hope you will be voting for me."

You shrink into your seat. You know it's your job to investigate all kinds of creatures but there's something about vampires you find especially unnerving.

"Put me down as undecided," says Klaus. "I'll have to see who else is on the ballot paper."

"No one of any consequence, I assure you."

"At the moment I'm trying to discover what's happened to Dr Franklefink's Monster Maker."

"Oh, that old thing," says Stoker with a smile. "The man is paranoid. Franklefink wants to create life but we vampires have no interest in mere mortal matters. It's probably one of the children who attended that party – not mine, of course – or those wretched witches. It certainly wouldn't be an upstanding member of the community such as I. If you ask me, Franklefink is just trying to damage my chances in the election."

"Why would he want to do that?" asks Klaus.

"The Franklefinks have never warmed to me," said Stoker. "I can't think why. I'm sorry. The lights have changed! Just as our community will change once I've been voted in as Night Mayor. Good luck with your investigation."

Before Klaus can respond, Stoker drives off. A car behind you beeps its horn. Stoker turns left. Klaus continues straight on.

"Stoker is an ambitious man," says Klaus. "And if Dr Franklefink has some kind of grudge against him, that could be a vital clue. How is his campaign to be Night Mayor relevant? I can't see how it gives him an obvious motive to steal the Monster Maker."

You're listening but you're also looking at your notes in case there's something Klaus has missed. It's time to decide what to do but, once again, you're in two minds about what to say.

? "I think we should go to the school and talk to some of Monty's party guests."
Turn to page 39
HAVENTRY SCHOOL FOR THE UNUSUALLY GIFTED

? "Let's go and talk to the witches from the catering company."
Turn to page 66
THE WITCHES' OVEN

THE WITCHES' OVEN

BURNELLA AND BRIDGET MILKBIRD RUN the Witches' Oven out of an old caravan. When it isn't roaming around town, it can be found parked on a patch of waste ground by the railway track. The commuters who catch the train to work never give it a second glance but Klaus has encountered them before and he knows just how to find them. You leave Watson on the road and walk towards the caravan.

As you near it, you see that it's rocking with movement and you can hear the whir of electric whisks and the sizzle of pans. Listening carefully, you identify more sinister sounds, such as buzzing chainsaws, cackling laughter and bloodcurdling screams.

You knock on the door, then shuffle closer to your boss, not wanting to show your nerves.

When there's no reply, you knock louder. This time it goes quiet and the caravan stops rocking.

"Who is it?" calls a croaky voice.

"We're busy," adds another.

"Klaus Solstaag – and assistant." He gives you what he probably thinks is a reassuring pat on the back, but it's so hard that it almost takes your breath away. "We have a couple of questions."

"Hold on!"

"Yes, wait a minute."

The voices have a panicked quality as the witches chatter between themselves.

itches
Ov

"No, just put the lid on it... It doesn't matter if it congeals."

"But it's bubbling over."

"Then turn it down."

The door swings open to reveal the grubbiest witch you've ever seen. It isn't just the twigs in her hair – she has a filthy face and overalls covered in an array of colourful stains too.

"My sister and I are very busy," she says.

A second witch appears next to the first. "What does he want, Bridget?"

"I can't read minds, can I, Burnella?"

"Excuse *me* for thinking that a witch might actually be able to do some magic!" In one hand Burnella is holding a small cauldron. In the other, she's holding a disembodied hand.

"That's an interesting-looking wand," says Klaus.

"This?" squawks Burnella, holding up the hand. "Bridget misunderstood when I asked her to hand me some nails." She laughs.

"My colleague and I are here about a recent theft," says Klaus.

Bridget turns to look at you. Her eyes are full of mischief as she leans forwards. You feel as though your feet are wedged in blocks of ice. You look down to check whether they actually are – you never know with witches – but it's not magic that grips you. It's fear.

"There's more to this one than meets the eye," she says, peering at you. "This one has unexpected power."

You don't know what she means by this, but the way she seems to be able to look inside your mind unnerves you and makes your brain itch. You're grateful when Klaus steps in front of you to block her gaze.

"Never mind my assistant," says Klaus. "We're here about what happened yesterday."

"What happened yesterday, Bridget?" asks Burnella.

"The brat's party," says Bridget.

"That's right," replies Burnella. "The brat's party."

"Mind if we come in?" Klaus doesn't wait for an answer. He steps inside the caravan, pushing past the witches.

"Hey, watch it," says Bridget.

"You big hairy lummox," adds Burnella.

Nervously, you follow him in. Lying in the middle of the caravan on a fold-down bed, with a white sheet over its body, is an enormous lifeless monster. Its taut skin is covered in stitches. It has one hand missing and it's totally bald.

"How interesting," says Klaus. "Here we are looking for a missing Monster Maker and I find you, two of our prime suspects, with a monster."

"Pure coincidence," says Bridget.

"Happenchance," adds Burnella.

"You sound as though you already knew it was missing," Klaus points out, noticing that the witches don't seem at all surprised to learn of the theft.

"Word travels pretty fast around here," says Bridget. "But don't go thinking we took it, because you're barking up the wrong caravan. We're just making Brian here to help us in the kitchen."

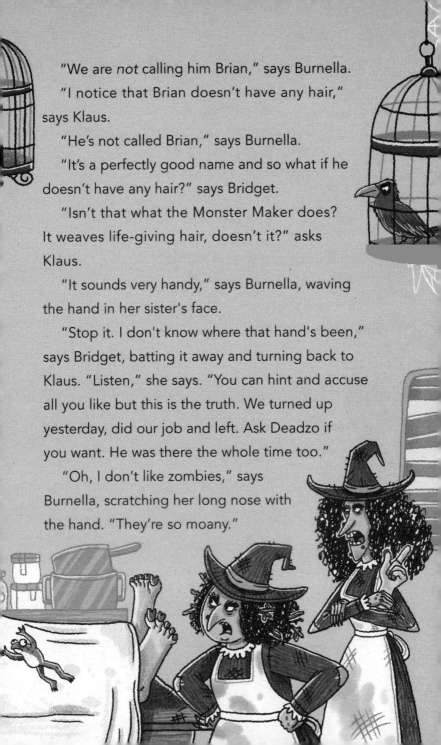

"We are *not* calling him Brian," says Burnella.

"I notice that Brian doesn't have any hair," says Klaus.

"He's not called Brian," says Burnella.

"It's a perfectly good name and so what if he doesn't have any hair?" says Bridget.

"Isn't that what the Monster Maker does? It weaves life-giving hair, doesn't it?" asks Klaus.

"It sounds very handy," says Burnella, waving the hand in her sister's face.

"Stop it. I don't know where that hand's been," says Bridget, batting it away and turning back to Klaus. "Listen," she says. "You can hint and accuse all you like but this is the truth. We turned up yesterday, did our job and left. Ask Deadzo if you want. He was there the whole time too."

"Oh, I don't like zombies," says Burnella, scratching her long nose with the hand. "They're so moany."

"Deadzo is on our list of suspects," says Klaus.

"Fascinating," says Burnella. "And *you're* on our list of people to turn into lizards."

"Lizards." Bridget tuts. "How very imaginative. Why not go the whole hog and turn them into frogs? What a cliché."

"And you're so original, are you?" asks Burnella. "What would you turn them into?"

"Another caravan?" says Bridget.

The caravan rocks violently in response.

"Don't be so sensitive, Susan," says Bridget, patting the side of the caravan. She turns to her sister. "Oh, I know. What about a bit of pavement?"

"A bit of pavement?" squawks Burnella.

"Oh, it must be horrible being a bit of pavement," says Bridget. "People walking on you, dropping stuff on you and treading chewing gum into your face. Not to mention the dog poo."

"I see what you mean," says Burnella. "Yes, get out before we turn you into a bit of pavement." She waves her arms and suddenly you're both standing outside, even though you haven't moved a muscle. The caravan door slams shut.

"Witches," Klaus mutters.

You're too shaken to respond but you're glad to be

out of that caravan. You make your way across the waste ground to where Watson is faithfully awaiting your return.

"Good boy," says Klaus, tapping the car's roof.

Watson growls and gives a little wheel spin to show he's excited to see his master.

You get into the car, thinking through everything that just happened. If the witches are making a monster then they certainly have a strong motive for stealing the doctor's machine, but there are still pieces of the puzzle you have yet to uncover.

"So," says Klaus. "Next, I think we either pay Deadzo a visit or we get back to the office and take stock of where we're at."

You reply:

? "Let's get back to the office and review the evidence."

Turn to page 86

A LITTLE RESEARCH

? "We need to speak to Deadzo."

Turn to page 80

DEADZO THE ZOMBIE CLOWN

THE DOCTOR'S SHOPPING TRIP

YOU'VE COME TO A RATHER grey shopping centre, full of very ordinary-looking people. You marvel at how Klaus manages to go unnoticed in places like this.

"There's a knack to remaining undercover when you're trailing a suspect," he explains. "Look at me. I'm over two metres tall and covered in white fur. As far as most folk are concerned, I'm mythical, fictional and – my personal favourite – abominable. And yet I never get seen. Why?"

Klaus doesn't wait for an answer. "Because I don't act like I'm trying to hide," he says. "It's called *hiding in plain sight*. No one in this shopping centre is expecting to see a yeti, so no one sees a yeti. Even if they do give me a second glance, they dismiss me as a tall hairy man in a fur coat."

It's true that none of the shoppers bats an eyelid as you pass. The doctor is clearly not expecting anyone to be watching him either. You've stayed on his trail from his house to this shopping centre without him turning his head once. You've witnessed him buy a lab coat, pick up a new set of test tubes and get a haircut – although in your opinion, his hair looked even messier on the way out of the barbershop than it did on the way in.

"The doctor hired us," says Klaus, "but that doesn't put him above suspicion. Everyone has secrets: the doctor, me ... even you have a few, I expect."

Klaus's running commentary is cut short when Dr Franklefink emerges from a shoe shop and starts walking towards you. "Quick, he's coming this way! In here."

Klaus pushes you into a clothes shop. You dive behind a rail while he ducks down, removes his hat and hides among a rack of coats. The doctor doesn't notice either of you as he hurries past.

Klaus stands up straight again and you both follow the doctor to the lift.

"He must be going back to his car," says Klaus. "We'll have to take the stairs."

There are a lot of stairs. The doctor parked his car on level seven. While Klaus climbs the stairs in easy bounds, it's harder work for you. By the time you reach the right floor, you're gasping. You try to get your breathing under control as Klaus opens the door. The doctor's car is there but there's no sign of him.

"Strange," says Klaus. "You'd expect him to have beaten us here. I wonder what's delayed him. I'd better keep watch on the car. You go and check the other floors, just in case."

The last thing you want to do is run up or down more stairs, but you do as you're told. The first couple of floors you try are empty but when you reach a level with a machine to pay for parking you hear a voice say, "Who's there?" Dr Franklefink's words echo off the concrete walls and make you jump.

You duck down. Has he seen you?

"Sorry. Did I give you a scare, Dr Franklefink?" a second voice replies.

You poke your head above the bonnet of a car and spot a tall gentleman with angular cheekbones and a perfectly bald head. He's holding a walking stick with an ornate silver handle. He carefully avoids a beam of sunlight from a gap in the wall as he approaches Dr Franklefink.

"Bramwell Stoker," says the doctor. "I know very well you took my Monster Maker. You will be revealed soon enough as the crook you are."

The vampire's thin lips curl into a dismissive smirk. "Where's your proof?"

"There are bat droppings in my lab," snaps the doctor.

"That doesn't sound very sanitary. Maybe you should hire that unicorn cleaning service. It's amazing how useful their horns are for cleaning out troublesome nooks and crannies."

"Never mind Uni-Clean. Mr Solstaag will prove you stole it."

"You've hired the yeti?" replies Stoker, with a note of irritation in his voice.

"Yes, and soon everyone will know you're a thief."

"I promise, hand on my heart, that I didn't take it."

"Your heart is as cold and dead as the rest of you. I know you did it and soon everyone else will too."

The vampire emits a low chuckle that grows into an evil guffaw. "You think I'm scared of you? In spite of you, I will be elected Night Mayor. Then the Shady Side of Haventry will be mine!"

With a clap of his hands, the vampire transforms into a swarm of bats that swirl like a tornado, then fly directly at the doctor.

"Get away! Leave me alone!" yells Franklefink.

The bats don't torment him for long, instead fluttering out into the sky. The doctor doesn't linger either.

"Horrible flapping creatures," he mutters under his breath, as he checks there aren't any left in his hair.

You stay hidden as he walks to the elevator and presses a button. There's plenty to digest in what you just heard and you mull it over as you wait. The lift door pings open and Franklefink steps inside. Once he's gone, you head back to the stairs. By the time you reach Klaus, the doctor's car is heading down the slope, out of the car park.

"He just left." Klaus greets you. "He must have been paying for his parking, I suppose. Shall we go and check out the school to question the other kids who were at the party?"

You hesitate to answer.

"Unless you saw something. Did you?" says Klaus.

Usually, you and your boss don't keep secrets from one another. He trusts you with so many of the decisions, but you wonder what would happen if you kept this latest discovery to yourself. Maybe you might be the one to solve the mystery this time. You could prove yourself to him.

"Well?" he says. "Did you?"

? Do you want to tell Klaus what you witnessed?

Turn to page 61
THE NIGHT MAYOR

? Or should you keep quiet about what you've learned?

Turn to page 39
HAVENTRY SCHOOL FOR THE UNUSUALLY GIFTED

DEADZO THE ZOMBIE CLOWN

HAVENTRY HAS TWO THEATRES. THE Royal Theatre is the sort of venue that puts on pantomimes starring minor celebrities who can't really sing and local DJs who can't really act.

And then there's Brockley Jacks, a cramped space above a pub where you can see fire-gargling, imp-racing or dragon-wrestling. Klaus asks an ogre downstairs where you can find Deadzo. The ogre points at the staircase. At the top, you find the zombie clown sitting on his own in a dressing room filled with partly deflated balloons and oversized props.

"Deadzo," says Klaus, "I have a couple of

questions about the children's party yesterday."

"Children's party," mutters Deadzo. "You know you've hit rock bottom when you're reduced to playing for children. All they want are fake flowers that shoot out water and people tripping up. What do children know about the noble art of clowning? Grimaldi himself once complimented my tumble."

"Who?" asks Klaus.

"Grimaldi, the great Victorian clown. He was a good friend of mine back when I had *live* performances."

"You're still performing," says Klaus.

"I mean 'live' as in *alive*," says the clown. "Back when I was a live clown, I performed for kings and queens. I played in palaces and state openings. Back then, I was valued, but dead clowning isn't the same.

There's barely a place for living clowns these days, let alone dead ones. And so, here I am in this … this…" He glances at you then says through gritted teeth, "This theatre."

"Yes, I can see the downside of being dead," says Klaus.

"Even the other clowns turn up their red noses at me. Oh, and the brains." Deadzo pulls a face of disgust. "Do you have any idea how revolting brains are? They really get stuck in your teeth. Also, they're hard to find when you spend all your time with actors."

"Talking of brains," says Klaus, with a wry smile, "I'm here to pick yours. We're investigating the disappearance of Dr Franklefink's Monster Maker."

"I hope you aren't suggesting I could have been involved in its removal," replies Deadzo.

"I've no reason to think that … yet." Klaus pauses to emphasize the word. "I don't suppose you've ever been accused of thieving before, have you?"

"Me? A thief?" says Deadzo. "The only thing I've ever stolen is the limelight … and the audience's hearts. Of course, in the world of dead clowning, there's always going to be rivalry and people will say the most awful things, but I try to rise above such pettiness. As the poet wrote, *Haters gonna hate*."

Deadzo swings round in his chair to face the mirror, then touches up his make-up with a small brush. The red around his mouth is smudged and he carefully colours it in again.

"So, yesterday's performance," says Klaus. "How did it go?"

"A children's party is less a performance, more a fight for survival. Those vile little things were running everywhere."

"I'm guessing you had a lot of equipment with you," continues Klaus. "How can I be certain you didn't carry out the Monster Maker, concealed among it all?"

Deadzo spins around and leans forwards, locking

eyes with your boss. You're pleased he isn't staring at you like that.

"Because I did not take it," he says firmly.

He sounds sincere enough but Klaus says, "You are an actor, though, aren't you?"

"I am." Deadzo turns back around in his chair and continues to fix his make-up. "If I were going to act the thief, I would act it superbly. But I've always been a scrupulously honest person. I suppose it's telling lies for a living that's made me such."

"Telling lies for a living?" echoes Klaus.

"Acting," says Deadzo. "Through lies we find truth."

"Sounds like our job," retorts Klaus. "You saw nothing suspicious?"

"I witnessed no theft. If I were to point an accusing finger, I would probably point it at one of those children. Younglings, in my experience, are usually up to no good. And not one of them gave my act the attention it so richly deserved." The clown scowls at you. "Now, I have a performance of my award-winning solo show this evening. I must prepare." He lets out a long sigh, then begins making strange noises to warm up his vocal cords.

"Hommmmmmm... Meeee... Meeee... Youuu... Youuu... Byeeeeeeee... Byeeeeeee..."

You take the stairs back down through the pub and out into the street. You glance at your notes, which detail where you've been, who you've spoken to and what you've learned. Klaus is by your side, always eager to move on to the next thing. But sometimes you need a moment to reflect: to try to see the bigger picture.

? If you haven't already been back to your office to review the evidence you've gathered so far, go now!

Turn to page 86

A LITTLE RESEARCH

? If you've already been back to the office, return to school. It's pick-up time!

Turn to page 93

HOME TIME

A LITTLE RESEARCH

You're back in your messy office, staring at the list of suspects in your notebook. Next to the names you wrote down this morning, you've added possible motives and made a note of all the clues you've gathered. Every single person at the party would have had the opportunity to steal the Monster Maker. How can you work out who's guilty?

"Sometimes it helps to look away from the page," says a reassuring voice behind you.

Your boss is standing behind you, looking over your shoulder. As he squints at your notes, he lowers his head so that his fine white hairs tickle the back of your neck. "I've just left a message for Chief

Inspector Darka. I don't miss working for the UPF but they can access certain information that's trickier to obtain as a private investigator. Also, I've been doing some research. Take a look."

A pile of newspapers lands on your desk with a *THUD!*

"I've been going through back copies of the *Haventry News of the Unusual* to confirm what I thought. I knew Bramwell Stoker had run for Night Mayor before but I hadn't realized he's put his name forward in every election for the past two hundred years." He smiles. "And get this: he's never been elected."

You flick through a few pages, reading the headlines.

Stoker Stokes Up New Campaign
Stoker Fails Again
Stoker: The Bald Truth

"Listen to this one." Klaus reads out an article. *"A recent survey of the Shady Side community*

Stoker: The Bald

suggests that Bramwell Stoker's repeated failure to win may be down to his baldness. Stoker has sucked the blood out of this constituency for two centuries, making him perfect material for a life in politics, and yet sixty-two per cent of Shady Side residents cited 'baldness' as their main reason for voting for another candidate."

Klaus slams his large hairy hand down on the desk, then picks up another newspaper.

"And guess who will be running against him in this election? Only our old friend Dr Franklefink.

He mentioned that he'd be at the City Chamber this evening. I didn't question it because a lot of our community will be down there for the debate. I had no idea he was standing as a candidate this time."

You're wondering what any of this has to do with the theft of the Monster Maker but Klaus is one step ahead.

"If Stoker stole it, Franklefink would want his name to be revealed in public. That would explain why he wanted us to meet him there. Could this be a case of political mud-slinging? But if it is, who's slinging mud at whom?"

It's a good question and you wish you had a good answer.

"Also, I found some reviews of Deadzo's most recent shows," adds Klaus. "They're like a stormy night in Haventry: bleak and not a star in sight." He chuckles at his own joke. "But I did find one previous theft. A few years ago, Deadzo was accused of stealing another clown's face."

You're just about to ask what that means when Klaus continues.

"It says here that clowns all have different looks, and that another zombie clown by the name of Bango claimed that Deadzo stole his look." Klaus is interrupted by the phone ringing.

He answers it. "Shady Side Investigations, Private Investigator Klaus Solstaag speaking... Ah, Darka. Thanks for getting back to me. I've got a few names I'd like to run past you, if you don't mind. Are any of these people on your records at UPF?"

Klaus is still on good terms with his old boss, a minotaur called Chief Inspector Darka. He reads out the suspect list, then listens, grunting and nodding as he scribbles notes on the pad. When he's finished, he hangs up and turns back to you.

"Hm, not as much as I'd hoped but a few morsels worth considering," he says. "First up, the goblin twins. Known to the UPF for ruckus-making, havoc-wreaking and general disruption. No mention of theft, though, unlike Huey Cry, who's been accused of stealing chickens by several nearby farmers. But his file is nothing like the one they've got on the witches. Those two have been accused of everything from kidnapping to grand theft, looting, turning people into unnatural things and going through a red light on a broomstick."

You're trying to keep a note of everything, but Klaus is speaking quickly and he expects you to keep up.

"There's nothing much out of the ordinary on the others, although Bramwell Stoker has been interviewed about a number of missing people over the years. But that's hardly surprising for a vampire…"

He runs a fingernail down his notes, grunting to himself, then looks up and says, "This might be something. The UPF's records go a long way back and I asked Darka to delve into our ghost's history. Apparently Lana was killed the same night Dr Franklefink's great-great-grandfather brought his first-ever monster to life. Interesting coincidence or key clue? Who knows?"

He smiles. You can tell he's enjoying himself. As he's

explained before, when you're in the middle of a mystery it's as though you're standing in the centre of a storm. If you can find that perfectly calm spot, then you'll be able to see clearly what's happening around you.

"So, we have another choice to make."

? If you haven't already, do you want to go and talk to Deadzo the zombie clown?

Turn to page 80
DEADZO THE ZOMBIE CLOWN

? Or do you want to go to the school? It's pick-up time!

Turn to page 93
HOME TIME

HOME TIME

IT'S PICK-UP TIME WHEN YOU arrive at Haventry School for the Unusually Gifted. You're about to get out of Watson when Klaus stops you.

"I think we should keep our distance here. Asking questions can get you answers but suspects act differently when they're being interviewed. Let's watch how things unfold when we don't get involved." Klaus pats the dashboard and his voice softens. "There's a good boy, Watson. Settle."

Watson has noticed a car with Bramwell Stoker's grinning face on the top and the words: *VOTE FOR STOKER! YOU CAN COUNT ON ME.* It parks on the zigzag lines by a sign that reads: *DO NOT PARK.*

Across the road, a green Volvo is pulling in between Ma Squelch's truck and Dr Franklefink's hatchback.

"Keep your head down and watch carefully," says Klaus.

You push yourself lower into the seat. You're close enough to see Mrs Cry leave her car to join Ma Squelch and Dr Franklefink at the gates. Bramwell Stoker's car is much closer to the school gates than the others. He extends a long black umbrella before cautiously stepping out.

"You aren't allowed to park there," says Dr Franklefink.

"I'll park where I see fit," replies the vampire. "I remember this road before they painted the lines. I was here before it was a road."

"Being two hundred years old doesn't give you any special rights. When I'm Night Mayor I'll increase the fines for such anti-social behaviour," announces Dr Franklefink.

"You? The Night Mayor of Haventry? Don't make me laugh," retorts Stoker.

"I've never voted for no Night Mayor cos there's never been anyone worth voting for," says Ma Squelch, who has at least three of her grandchildren – or grand-gobbles as she calls them – hanging off her.

"Er, my name has always been on the ballot paper," says Stoker.

"Exactly," says Ma Squelch.

"I do urge you to vote for me, then," replies Dr Franklefink. "The *bald* truth of the matter is—"

"How dare you?" interrupts Stoker. "You, sir, are bald-ist."

"I think you'll find *you* are the one who is baldest." The doctor snorts at his own joke. "And you will soon be revealed as a thief and a liar."

"What? For stealing your pathetic device?"

"I know it was you!" Dr Franklefink raises his voice. "The bat droppings at the scene of the crime are all the proof we need."

"*Pooh* to your poo. It wasn't me."

"How dare you?" The doctor approaches Bramwell, but Mrs Cry holds him back. The doctor tries to wrestle free but Mrs Cry doesn't release her grip until he gives up. She's clearly stronger than she looks.

"Pity," snorts Ma Squelch. "I like a good punch-up."

"You should be ashamed of yourselves, acting like this at the school gate," says Mrs Cry.

The children are starting to appear from inside the school now, and other parents are gathering. A pixie mum and an elf dad wave to their ogre daughter, who runs and hugs them, almost crushing them with her enormous arms. A sprite mum zips above the crowd and waves to her children, who fly up to meet her, then lob their bookbags at her.

"Pick up your wrappings, darling," says a mummified dad to his son. "You're coming unravelled."

Amidst the throng, you spot Monty's distinctive purple hair. He is having an intense conversation with Bobby Stoker, but you can't hear what they're saying. Huey walks alone. Right at the back, the goblin twins tumble, trip and hop towards the school gates, while Lana the ghost drifts sadly above them all.

"Come on, Monty," calls Dr Franklefink. "Stop chatting and let's go."

"Can Bobby come over to play?" asks Monty.

"No," replies his father.

"But he's my best friend," protests Monty.

You open your notebook, circling the names Monty and Bobby as you consider whether their friendship is relevant to this mystery.

"Sorry, son, but that's just the way it is. Besides, I have work to do – valuable, vital work!" he cries. "Science is my passion. The pursuit of perfection is my goal!"

"Da-ad," says Monty, clearly embarrassed by his father.

"And I will not rest until whoever stole my Monster Maker –" he pauses to glare at Stoker – "is brought to justice."

"Dad. Stop, please."

As Monty tugs on his father's sleeve, trying to pull him away, you wonder if his tone reveals more than mere embarrassment. Is he hiding something?

"Maybe I should come over another time, Monty," says Bobby.

"When I am Night Mayor," proclaims Bramwell Stoker, "I shall make it compulsory to invite vampires into homes."

"I wish you'd stop running for election every year," says Bobby. "You're always so grouchy when you lose."

"I shall not lose this time," replies his father. He opens the car door for his son. "Not when I have such weak competition," he adds with a parting glance at Dr Franklefink.

"Why, you—" snarls Dr Franklefink, but the Stokers get into the car and slam the doors shut.

"Vote for Stoker," booms Bramwell's voice from the speaker on top.

"That rotten, no good—"

The doctor swings around to find Mrs Cry standing behind him. "Ah, Trisha. Of course, Huey is welcome to come around any time."

"That's very kind," she replies. "Perhaps another time. We have plans this evening. Don't we, darling?" She kisses Huey's head, causing his cheeks to redden.

"Do you have to make it sound so ordinary?" he says. "It's the full moon tonight."

"Yes, it's funny that the one time you would fit in around here is the one time none of us see you," says Monty.

You can't tell if that was meant to sound as mean as it did but there's no mistaking the mortified look on Huey's face.

"Ordinary, ordinary," chant the goblins. "Huey is ordinary."

"I am not," states Huey. "I'm a were—"

"Now, darling," his mother interrupts him. "I don't think we need to broadcast the details of our monthly inconvenience. There's nothing wrong with being ordinary. Come on, say goodbye to your friends."

"Bye, Monty," says Huey. "Bye, Grinola and Grundle."

The goblins are the last to leave because Ma Squelch has to keep rounding them up. Every time she gets one back in the truck, another one escapes. Eventually she entices them back in with the words: "We're going to Creepy Pete's for pizza tonight!"

"Yay!" cry the goblins.

Once everyone has gone and a giant dung beetle has locked the school gates, Klaus starts Watson's engine and you head back to the office.

"There's a lot to mull over," says Klaus. "As I said, when you get a chance to observe your suspects without their knowledge, they reveal a lot more of themselves than when you're there. Let's get back to the office and work out what to do next."

Klaus falls silent on the drive. He's deep in thought, busily processing all the facts and details he's gathered. You know you should be doing the same. He relies on you so much and you don't want to let him down. Besides, you've seen things from a different perspective to his, a human perspective. Perhaps you've picked up clues that he hasn't yet considered. You're keen to solve this mystery but you don't want to rush to a conclusion and end up missing something.

You take a deep breath and close your eyes. Another decision awaits you soon. But first you need to whittle down the suspects.

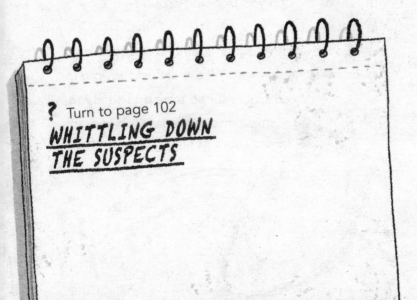

? Turn to page 102
WHITTLING DOWN THE SUSPECTS

WHITTLING DOWN THE SUSPECTS

KLAUS LEANS BACK ON HIS chair. He tries to chew on a pencil, but it snaps with the first bite. You've been poring over the facts for hours now and it's beginning to feel as though you're going around in circles.

"So let's go through it again." Klaus spits out splinters as he speaks. "All the children on our suspect list had the opportunity to sneak into the lab during the game of hide-and-seek."

Klaus looks around for another pencil. You hide the one you're using.

"Is it me or is it getting hot in here?" he asks.

You're pretty sure it's him. The office is like a fridge but you're well accustomed to your boss's love of the cold. He turns on a fan and sticks his face in front of it.

"That's better," he says. "So, where were we?"

You show him your notes, listing the suspects, the motives and all the clues you've picked up on so far.

"Bobby Stoker appears to be Monty's closest friend, yet their fathers are political rivals," says Klaus.

Failing to locate another pencil, he grabs a thick felt-tip and scrawls *STOKER* on one wall and *FRANKLEFINK* on another. You're quite used to this kind of behaviour. Klaus's methods are as unconventional as his cleaning costs are high, but they get the job done. He stands in the middle of the room, arms outstretched, pointing at both names.

"Monty has access to the Monster Maker all the time, so why would he want to steal it and why during his own party? Also, Dr Franklefink was making Enormelda as a mother for him. Why would he remove the one thing that made that possible?"

He begins to write *Enormelda* on the wall but gets confused about how many 'm's there are and gives up.

"We should also consider all the things his father didn't tell us when he employed us. Why didn't he mention that he was running against Bramwell Stoker to become the Night Mayor of Haventry? He's had Stoker in his sights since the start – and there is the bat poo to consider. Is it hard evidence or a red herring?"

Klaus puts a second fan on. Unlike him, you don't have a thick layer of fur to keep you warm. You tuck your arms into your coat and blow into your hands to warm them up.

"Next," he says, "the werewolves." Klaus writes WEREWOLF in block capitals beneath a painting of an iceberg that hangs above his desk. "Mrs Cry is about as respectable as they come, while Huey does have a history of stealing. But if it was him, how would he have removed the Monster Maker from the party without his mother finding out? And just as importantly, *why* would he take it? What possible use might he have for such a thing?"

Klaus scratches his head.

"Next, Lana the ghost… She's the only party guest who doesn't have an adult to keep tabs on her."

Klaus writes *GOST* on the window, steps back, looks at it critically, then adds the missing 'h'. Each stroke of the pen makes a squeaking noise that goes right through you.

"What might Lana's motive be? What would a ghost want to bring to life?"

You scribble notes as you listen.

"Remember, she died on the night the first Franklefink monster was created. Is that significant? We certainly can't rule her out yet."

He draws a large circle around the word GHOST, making another horrendous SQUEAK!

"Which brings us to the goblins."

Klaus stomps across the room, writes GOBLINS on the door, then turns on yet another fan.

"The Squelches have been in trouble with the law before, and if this was a UPF investigation, you can bet that they'd be the first hauled in for questioning. But we can afford to be a bit more broadminded in our approach."

Klaus stands at the centre of the room, with four fans turned on to full blast. Bits of paper are flying everywhere. You're trying to keep yourself warm in these Arctic conditions while also

checking your notes in case there's something you've picked up on that he's forgotten.

"So that's the partygoers. What about the rest? The first to arrive at the Franklefink house on the day of the robbery were the caterers." He writes THE WITCHES on a piece of paper. "Those two are a tricksy pair, all right. Could they be our thieves?"

You have an opinion on this but when your boss makes the office so cold, you find it difficult to talk through your chattering teeth.

"Next came Deadzo, the zombie clown. Children's entertainer isn't exactly his first choice of career, but how would the Monster Maker help?"

Klaus attaches a piece of paper to another fan. It has a clown face drawn on it. He turns to you for an answer and finally notices that you're shivering.

"Oh, I'm sorry," he says.

He switches off the fans, then lumbers over and grabs you in a big yeti hug. You feel your blood warm up and thoughts return to your head.

"So, it's time to pick a path," says Klaus.

"Taking into account everything I've just said and everything we've learned, who do you think took the Monster Maker?"

Do you think it was one of the children?

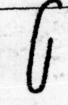

? Bobby Stoker, the vampire

Turn to page 110
VISITING VAMPIRES

? Monty Franklefink, the monster

Turn to page 156
MAYBE MONTY

? Huey Cry, the werewolf

Turn to page 124
CRY OUT LOUD

? Grundle and Grinola Squelch, the goblins

Turn to page 118
CREEPY PETE'S PIZZERIA

? Or Lana, the ghost

Turn to page 129
NO REST

Or are you leaning towards it being one of the grown-ups?

? Bramwell Stoker. the vampire

Turn to page 110

VISITING VAMPIRES

? Bridget and Burnella Milkbird, the witches

Turn to page 135

MILKBIRDS' MONSTER

? Deadzo, the zombie clown

Turn to page 183

THE MONSTER'S HAIR

? Or perhaps even Dr Franklefink himself

Turn to page 150

CONFRONTING FRANKLEFINK

VISITING VAMPIRES

AS KLAUS STOPS THE CAR outside the Stokers'
imposing family residence, Watson growls quietly.
He sounds scared. You know how he feels. There's
something about this place that makes you want to
turn and run for your life.

"Quiet now, boy," says Klaus, tapping the
dashboard. "It's all right."

Watson falls silent and Klaus continues in a
whisper.

"If we suspect either of these vampires of having
taken the Monster Maker, the first thing we need
to do is check whether it's in the house."

Gazing up at the dark, gothic building,

it's as though the bricks are cemented together with a mix of fear and death. You've heard that vampires require an invitation to enter others' houses but you have no desire to step inside this intimidating structure, whether you're invited or not.

"If it is in there," continues Klaus, "they aren't exactly going to let us wander in and take a look. One of us needs to sneak in, while the other distracts them."

The way he smiles at you, you know what's coming next.

"Sorry," he says. "Yetis aren't really built for sneaking around. I'll keep them talking while you go in. As soon as I knock on the door, you'll have about five minutes to get in and see what you can find out. It shouldn't be a problem. Vampires don't usually need to worry too much about security. Are you ready?"

You nod. You try to appear calm, but your heart is already beating fast and your palms are sweaty. You're petrified at the prospect of breaking into a vampire's house but you swallow that fear and ready yourself.

"Don't worry," says Klaus. "As I always say, if you don't feel a few butterflies in your stomach, the chances are you aren't doing the job properly."

Klaus waits in the car while you get out and head down an alleyway that leads to the back of the house. It's so dark that even the shadows cast shadows. You hear a howl in the distance, then a growl much closer by. A flurry of bats bursts from a tree. It startles you. Is this why Klaus sent you? You've heard him say before that he doesn't like bats.

Whatever the reason, you have a job to do, so you pick up your pace. The Stokers' back gate is made from ornately woven black metal in the shape of a bat. You lift the latch and push it open.

CREEEAK!

The sound makes you jump.

You freeze, too scared to move, rigid with fear.

You step into the back garden and follow a winding path past hedges cut to look like strange animals. You spot a large kennel. You can hear something breathing heavily. Maybe snoring ... maybe not.

Walking cautiously, you reach the back door. You hear the doorbell ring and see a movement as someone goes to answer it. A small window is open. You find a plant pot to hitch yourself up. You get a foot on to a ledge and hoist yourself inside, scuffing your shins on the window frame. You land on the downstairs toilet. Fortunately the lid is down.

You can hear your boss at the front door.

"Mr Solstaag," says Bramwell Stoker.

"Hi, Klaus," says Bobby.

"I have a few questions," says Klaus.

"We were just about to have a little *nibble* of something. We've ordered a delivery. Why don't you join us?" says Bramwell.

"That's very kind but I think we have different dietary requirements," says Klaus. "This will only take five minutes."

This is it. You have to go now. The house is waiting to be explored but you don't have much time. You summon every bit of courage you have and tiptoe into the hall. Every floorboard creaks. Your boss develops a cough, rhythmic enough to time with your footsteps as you make your way down into the cellar.

"Are you all right, Mr Solstaag?" you hear Bramwell ask.

"Just –" cough – "a –" cough – "little –" cough – "furball."

His voice is muffled and distant now that you've reached the bottom of the stairs. Two coffins lie at opposite ends of the room. One is full size, the other is for a child. You spot sprinklings of brown pellets in one corner. Just like the bat poo found at the scene of the crime. Tattered hardback books are stacked beside the large coffin. A pile of comics lies by the smaller one. There's no sign of the Monster Maker.

You go back up and quickly cross the hallway to the stairs. This brings you close to Bramwell and Bobby Stoker. You hear them sniff as you pass behind them, picking up the scent of your blood.

"If that's all, we have to get on." Bramwell Stoker is losing patience with your boss.

"Also, I'm still undecided who to vote for in the election." Klaus blurts out the words. He's trying to buy you more time.

Suddenly he has Bramwell's full attention and you have your chance to go upstairs. You search the rooms as quickly as you can. Heavy curtains hang in front of the windows. There's very little in the way of furniture. If you didn't know someone lived here, you'd think the house was abandoned. There's no sign of the Monster Maker.

You hear footsteps coming up the stairs.

Panicking, you run to the window and pull back the curtain. You fiddle with the latch, then heave it open. There's a spindly tree outside. You think you can reach it if you jump.

You're about to make the leap when something catches your eye. Two streets away, you spot Huey Cry. He's carrying something but he's too far away to get a clear view. It's the right size to be the Monster Maker but you can't be sure. Maybe it's just a large chicken, or something else entirely.

It's impossible to know for certain and there is no time to stop and stare. You clamber out and close the window behind you. You don't want to leave any clue that you were there. Your hands are shaking as you make your way down the tree. You've climbed trees before but usually you start at the bottom and work up.

When you finally swing down and drop to the ground, you return to the car where Klaus is waiting for you. As soon as you're back in the car, you breathe a sigh of relief. Watson is keen to get going too – he starts moving before your boss has even turned the ignition.

"Welcome back," says Klaus. The air conditioning is on full blast, making it cold inside, but you're pleased to be back with your boss. "Any joy finding the Monster Maker in there?"

You shake your head.

"No, I guess it was a long shot," he says. "My interview was no more illuminating either. So whether or not the vampires are still on our suspect list, we need to follow up another lead for the moment. My feeling is that we should be checking in on the Franklefink residence, but it's your call."

You're still thinking about what you witnessed

out of the window. Did you just see Huey Cry clutching the very item you're searching for, or is your boss right that you should turn your attention to Dr Franklefink? A wrong move at this stage could endanger the investigation...

? Should you go with your boss's instincts and make Dr Franklefink your next stop?

Turn to page 150
CONFRONTING FRANKLEFINK

? Or will you tell Klaus what you just saw and get over to the Cry household immediately?

Turn to page 124
CRY OUT LOUD

CREEPY PETE'S PIZZERIA

MOST OF THE RESTAURANTS IN Haventry would go into instant meltdown were they suddenly overrun by a family of goblins, but Creepy Pete's Pizzeria is used to it. Located on the town's Shady Side, it's run by skeletons and has an unusual selection of diners.

"Welcome to Creepy Pete's Pizzeria! I'm Tony but can call me Bony Tony. I'll be your waiter today," says the skeleton who greets you at the door.

"I would *love* to eat," says Klaus, "but I'm here to talk to the goblins over there."

Had there been any colour in the waiter's face, it would have drained away. "Oh, the Squelches. Please say you've come to take them away."

"Why? What have they done?"

"What haven't they done! They chew on the furniture, fight with bread sticks and throw the dough balls… And, as you can see, we're running a *skeleton* staff at the moment."

A goblin leaps off the table and grabs a lampshade, swinging on it a couple of times before the whole thing comes away from the ceiling and crashes on to the table.

Klaus pats Tony sympathetically on the back and you walk over to the goblins.

Ma Squelch is splitting up a fight between Grundle and Grinola. "Why are you two always playing tricks on each other?" she says, grabbing a ketchup bottle and squirting it into both of their faces.

"I wonder where they get that from," mutters Klaus.

"Oh, it's you," says Ma Squelch, "and your silent sidekick. What do you want?"

"The same thing I always want – the truth," says Klaus. "Grundle and Grinola, if you know anything at all about the missing Monster Maker – and I very much get the feeling you do – then it's time to come clean."

"Uh-oh," says Grundle. "Is it bath night?"

"Bath night?" repeats Grinola.

"Bath night?" echo their siblings, jumping and shouting even more than before.

"QUIET!" The cry comes from the swing doors that lead to the kitchen. There stands a skeleton in a chef's hat, with a rolling pin in his right hand, whacking it against the bony palm of his left. "Listen, you Squelches," he yells. "This is a reputable restaurant. If you can't abide by my rules, you have to leave. No gnawing. No screaming. No jumping. No tricking. And definitely no licking. Now settle down and EAT YOUR PIZZA!"

The goblins jump back on to their seats and start stuffing bits of pizza into their mouths.

"Thank you," says the chef, going back into the kitchen.

"One question, Grinola," says Klaus. "Why did you steal the Monster Maker?"

"How did you know?" she says.

"Grinola!" moans Grundle. "He didn't. Not until you said that."

"Oh. Sorry," says Grinola. "But we didn't steal it first. We only stole it second."

"Stop talking!" Grundle grabs his sister's hand. "Remember what's written on your— Oh, it rubbed off. Still, we promised. And a goblin's promise is sacred."

"I thought that was elves," says Klaus.

"He's right. Elves' promises are sacred," says Ma Squelch. "Goblins usually lie through their teeth." She turns to face you and Klaus. "You asked your questions and you got enough answers from my grand-gobbles. But until you have proof, you can't pin nothing on us. We ain't got the Monster Maker, so be off with you."

There are certainly more questions to ask but your boss places a firm hand on your shoulder and you know it's time to go.

When you get outside the restaurant, Klaus is munching on a slice of pizza. You're unsure where he got it but the food has livened him up. His eyes are burning bright with excitement.

"You see this slice of pizza?" he says. "Looking at this, even though I don't have the rest, I can calculate how big it was, what kind it was and how generous the chef was with the toppings. I can tell you which side was left slightly too long in the hottest part of the oven and I could even make a guess about who ordered it."

He takes another bite.

"But, just as with a case like this, the longer you spend trying to connect the pieces, the harder it gets to see the whole picture." He shoves the remainder of the slice into his mouth. "In other words, we had better move on to the next person on the list."

You reply:

? "Let's go and visit Lana the ghost next."

Turn to page 129

NO REST

? "I think we'd better talk to Monty."

Turn to page 156

MAYBE MONTY

CRY OUT LOUD

IT'S NOT DARK YET BUT, as you turn into the quiet cul-de-sac where the Cry family lives, you notice that the perfectly round moon is peeking out from behind a cloud. You've always assumed that werewolves only come out at night, but if a full moon is visible during the day, does that count?

"Don't worry." Klaus picks up on your anxiety. "I'll keep you safe, but don't be surprised if you notice a few changes to Mrs Cry and her son."

At moments like this it's comforting that your boss is a seven-foot-tall yeti with limbs like tree trunks. He drops one arm over your shoulder, almost making your legs buckle, then raises the other and knocks on the door.

"Er, it's not a good time." You hear Mrs Cry's voice, but the door remains unopened.

"My assistant and I just want a quick word," says Klaus. "We've been on the trail of Dr Franklefink's missing Monster Maker all day and we have some questions."

Mrs Cry huffs and sighs, then opens the door but she keeps the chain on. Her face is still in human form but her eyes are wild and urgent. Her nose twitches and a droplet of saliva appears at the side of her mouth. She wipes it away.

"Please," she says. "It's getting late."

"We appreciate that," says Klaus. "It won't take long."

She closes the door. For a moment, you think she must have slammed it in your face but then she undoes the latch and opens it wide.

She doesn't look that different from when you last saw her at school pick-up, but there's definitely something wolfish about her twitching movements, and her hair looks tousled.

You notice the skin on her hands is pulsating. Something underneath is trying to push its way through the pores. She runs her fingers through her hair and doubles over in pain. As the surge passes, she stands up straight, brushes herself down and says, "I'm sorry, it's the moo … the mooo … the moon, you see. We won't change until it's dark but the moo … the moon is already full and that makes things a bit trickier."

"Where's your son, Mrs Cry?"

"Upstairs, but I'd rather he wasn't disturbed. Our monthly situation is much harder for the cubs. It's fresher. They are less used tooooo … tooo…" She gathers herself. "One becomes accustomed to it over time, but the change is much trickier for the young."

"And it must be hard, his being bullied at school. It can't be easy for a kid who only fits in with the rest of his classmates one day a month. Monty teased him about it, didn't he?"

"I don't knooooow," replies Mrs Cry.

Upstairs, you hear a door slam. Your boss glances at you. Mrs Cry is wracked by pain, incapable of doing or saying anything until it passes. Klaus takes his opportunity, bounding up the stairs two steps at a time.

You follow him but you are slower.

Halfway up, you feel something grab your ankle. You lose your footing and crash down on to the carpeted stairs. You put your palms out to ease your fall but the hand yanks you down and your chin bangs painfully on every step. You look up and see Klaus standing at the top. Mrs Cry is behind you. She has released you and is busily adjusting the buttons on her cardigan.

"He's gone," says Klaus. "He jumped out of the window."

"There's nothing unusual about that," says Mrs Cry curtly. "What don't you understand, Mr Solstaag? We are werewolves. There is a full moon in the sky. Jumping out of a window and running off is not an admission of guilt. Now, please, I must ask you to leave."

Klaus makes no further protest as Mrs Cry ushers you out of the house. She closes the door quietly but firmly with you on the other side.

"Are you OK?" asks Klaus.

You nod. You're bruised but you've felt worse.

"Good." Klaus looks relieved not to have to administer any serious sympathy. "That was all pretty suspicious," he says. "But I think that was just Mrs

Cry's maternal instincts you saw there."

You rub your chin. You didn't just see her maternal instincts. You felt them and they hurt.

"Werewolves can be pretty protective over their litters," continues Klaus. "But why did Huey suddenly bolt? And which lead should we chase up next?"

It's a good question and you're relieved that Klaus doesn't suggest pursuing Huey. You certainly don't fancy trying to catch a werewolf when there's a full moon – night-time or not. You look at your list, and two names jump out at you.

? "The goblins."
Turn to page 118
CREEPY PETE'S PIZZERIA

? "Lana, the ghost."
Turn to page 129
NO REST

NO REST

"GHOSTS ARE A MORBID LOT." Klaus stops the car outside the gates of Haventry cemetery. It isn't yet night, but the sky is darkening and the thick trees that grow around the graveyard create an ominous feeling of gloom. "If I came back as a ghost, you wouldn't find me hanging around graveyards," he says.

The thought of a ghost yeti both amuses and frightens you. You're glad your boss is very much alive. You feel safe by his side.

As you step out of the car, a cloud shifts to reveal the moon. A cold breeze chills you to the bone. You shudder and, from the way Watson shivers and whimpers, it seems you aren't the only one who's

129

scared. A scurrying sound in a hedge nearby makes you both jump.

"It's probably just a rat," says Klaus. "Or a ghost. Or a ghost rat. Whatever, let's go in."

Klaus tugs the gates, easily breaking the chain that was holding them shut. You follow him along the gravel path into the cemetery.

"You are trespassers and you trespass against us," hisses a voice.

A luminous figure emerges from behind a gravestone.

"Lana," says Klaus. "You know this graveyard is public property."

"It is locked at night for good reason," says Lana. "It's the only time my kind get any peace and quiet."

As she speaks, you become aware that there are more ghosts around. They're everywhere; lying on the ground, leaning against gravestones, lurking in the shadows.

"These stones are our beds," says Lana.

"I didn't think you were capable of sleep," says Klaus.

"Rest, then," sighs Lana.

You look at her gravestone. It reads:

REST IN PEACE
LANA MACCABE
1845–1852
TAKEN TOO SOON

"You di— er, passed away a long time ago," says Klaus. "Why do you still go to school?"

"What *should* I be doing with my time?" she snaps. "Going on beach holidays? Learning to tango? Watching reruns of sitcoms? Pah! I go to school as a ghost because I went to school when I was alive."

"*Taken too soon*," Klaus reads out. "Do you mind if I ask you how you died?"

"I prefer not to talk about it."

"It's our job to ask questions. We have a mystery to solve."

Lana sighs, shudders and then speaks. "It was early evening," she says. "I was at home playing with my dolls. I had such a lovely dolls' house. I think he liked it too. I think that's what drew him in."

"Him?" says Klaus. "Who?"

If she hears the question, she doesn't answer it. "People didn't lock their doors so much in those days. All he had to do was turn the handle and he was inside. 'Hoooome,' he said. He was pointing at the dolls' house." Lana smiles wistfully.

"The first Franklefink monster," says Klaus. "We knew you died on the night it was brought to life, but we didn't realize that—"

She finishes his sentence. "—it took my life. Yes.

Rotten thing. Curse all those Franklefinks. I wish they'd never made a single a monster … except for Monty. He's all right, I suppose."

Klaus takes a deep breath, then asks, "Did you take the Monster Maker, Lana? Did you take it out of some kind of revenge?"

Lana bursts out laughing. She clutches her sides and doubles over.

"What's so funny?" demands Klaus.

"You think I waited two hundred years, then took that stupid machine as revenge? How ridiculous would that be?"

"Being ridiculous doesn't mean it isn't true," says Klaus.

"Well, it isn't," says Lana. "I didn't take it."

"Then give us something to go on," says Klaus. "I find it very hard to believe you didn't see something during that game of hide-and-seek."

"Oh, all right. I did see Monty carry something into his room."

"Why didn't you tell me before?"

"I told you, I like Monty in spite of what he is. It's your job to find out who took it, not mine; but personally, I think it's more likely to be the witches.

You know they're making a monster, don't you?" she says. "Now, please leave me to rest in peace."

Lana sits down in front of her gravestone, head in hands. You can't tell if she has tears on her cheeks or if it's just that the dampness of the gravestone is visible through her transparent skin.

"It's time to go," Klaus says.

It breaks your heart to see this ghost still mourning herself after all these years. You follow your boss out of the graveyard, back to his quivering car.

"Let's get out of here," says Klaus, as he squeezes himself into the driver's seat.

But where should you go?

? Should you visit the witches?
Turn to page 135
MILKBIRDS' MONSTER

? Or would you rather talk to Monty?
Turn to page 156
MAYBE MONTY

MILKBIRDS' MONSTER

YOU DRIVE OVER TO THE wasteland where Bridget and Burnella Milkbird's caravan is usually parked, but it isn't there.

"They must be out selling street food in town," says Klaus. "We'll just have to keep driving around until we find them."

Your mind is buzzing as Klaus drives through the Shady Side streets in search of the caravan. You're not sure what to think. You have theories and ideas but it feels as though every time you're getting somewhere with one suspect, another one pops up looking even more likely than the last. As Klaus says, everyone has something to hide.

They all lie. Some deal in great big whoppers. Others try to sell you little white ones. But if you can find the right thread to pull, the lies all unravel in the end.

Finally, you spot the witches' caravan parked outside Brockley Jacks theatre, underneath a poster that reads:

UNDEAD FUNNY
The Life and Death
of a Clown
ONE NIGHT ONLY

"Hm, interesting, two lots of suspects in one place. Maybe it's a coincidence or maybe there's a connection."

You open your book and look at your notes on the clown and the witches. But now is not the time for mulling them over – there are urgent questions to be asked.

A light drizzle hangs in the air as you approach the caravan. The door is open and a small awning sticks out above a serving hatch. Next to this is a chalkboard. The menu has been scrawled in red chalk:

A. HOT FRDOG AND DFRIES
B. POISONOUS TOAD IN THE HOLE
C. VEGETARIAN MEAL
D. WARTS AND ALL SURPRISE
E. POTION B

You're surprised to see a large lumbering monster wearing a shower cap at the window, waiting to take your order.

"Hi there," says Klaus. "What's good?"

"Gooood," repeats the monster in a low moan.

"What's the vegetarian meal?"

"Vegetariaaaan," says the monster.

"Yes, the vegetarian." Your boss sounds impatient.

"Vegetariaaaaaaan."

Bridget appears and pushes him out of the way. "Oh, you are a useless oaf. Go and scrub the cauldron." Turning, she says, "What Boris is trying to tell you is that the vegetarian meal consists of one lightly roasted vegetarian... Oh, it's you, Klaus."

"Yes, it's me," says Klaus. "What's Potion B?"

"What?" Bridget looks at the board. "Burnella, you useless old hoochie-coocher."

The other witch springs up at the window. "Takes one to know one. What?"

"It's not supposed to say Potion B. It's supposed to be *Option* B."

"What does that mean?" asks Burnella, peering out of the hatch and examining the board.

"Poisonous toad in the hole," replies her sister, dragging her back inside the van.

"So Option E is Option B," clarifies Burnella.

"Yes."

"Oh, well, I didn't realize that."

"Option Beeeeeee." The monster wipes the board with a grubby-looking cloth.

Now that he's stepped out of the caravan you can see him at his full height. He's around the same size as Klaus but, while your boss's hair sticks up, the top of Boris's head is hidden under a shower cap. An idea strikes you. You snatch the cloth from his hand and drop it.

"Clothhhh," Boris moans as he bends over to pick it up. He looks uncomfortable doing so, and you can tell that he hasn't yet got used to his body. The shower cap slips. Boris rights himself, then adjusts the cap – but you've already seen what lies under it. He has a head of bright purple hair.

You catch your boss's eye. He noticed too.

"So what will it be?" asks Bridget. "Because if you're not ordering—"

Before anyone can say another word, the theatre doors open and a small but noisy crowd bursts out. It's the usual varied mix of people you'd expect in this part of town.

"Oh dear, talk about dialling it in," says a vampire in a white fur-lined jacket.

"Dialling it in? I don't think he even had the correct number. Speaking of which, shall I call a cab?" says an imp, pulling a mobile phone almost as big as him out of his pocket.

Behind them, two distinctly dead-looking clowns are stumbling, arm in arm, propping each other up and talking closely.

"Dreadful," says one.

"A disgrace to the art form, Bango," says the other. "I say, didn't he steal your make-up design?"

"He did indeed. The way I do my cheeks. He stole that, for all the good it did him. Honestly, what a performance. Do you know what he looked like, Bingo?"

"Say it, Bango. I know what you're going to say but say it. Say it."

"He looked like a living clown pretending to be a zombie clown."

The other slaps his large gloved hand on his friend's arm. "That is it. That is precisely it. Such a disappointment."

Klaus lowers his head and speaks quietly in your ear. "Interesting, eh? Deadzo may not be the world's greatest actor but there's one part he should be able to play well and that's a zombie."

A crowd has gathered around the witches' caravan, ordering food, laughing and generally getting in the way. You were ready to confront the sisters about the monster's hair colour but a thought has occurred to you. Could Deadzo be involved in this mystery too after all?

"What do you reckon?" says Klaus. "Pay Deadzo a visit or wait for the witches?"

You reply:
? "Yes, it must be the witches."
Turn to page 189
VISION IN A CARAVAN

? "We need to talk to Deadzo."
Turn to page 142
NOT-SO DEADZO

NOT-SO DEADZO

YOU FIND DEADZO THE ZOMBIE clown sitting in his dressing room. His one-man show is over. From the look on his face and the comments you heard from his audience on the way out, it was not a success. He's staring at his own reflection. A meagre bunch of flowers lies in front of him.

"Do you know the hardest thing about being an old performer?" he says.

"The lack of money?" guesses Klaus.

"No, it isn't that. It isn't the uncertainty or the endless rejection. The hardest thing is admitting that the world was right. I was never good enough."

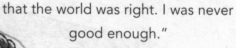

"You shouldn't be so hard on yourself," says Klaus. "It's only one bad show."

"One bad career is closer to the truth," says the clown dramatically. "I've done nothing but rebound from one bad decision to the next, like a brightly coloured pinball. And now I will fall through the flippers, unflipped, unloved and…" Deadzo pulls a large spotty handkerchief from his pocket. "Unnoticed."

"Things could still turn around for you." Klaus sounds genuinely concerned.

A flower in Deadzo's pocket perks up and he almost raises a smile, but the smile fades and the flower wilts. "No, I think not. I thought I had the answer but, yet again, I fear, I have stumbled into another terrible decision."

"What was the answer, Deadzo?" asks Klaus. "What did you do?"

The clown picks up the bunch of wilted roses.

"Bango was there in the crowd to witness my failure tonight. I'll bet he loved every minute."

"That's the clown who accused you of stealing his face," says Klaus.

"Yes," says Deadzo miserably. "I feel like such a fool. All these years as a zombie clown, I spent so much time yearning for what I used to be, I never appreciated what I had become."

"I'm not quite following," says Klaus.

Deadzo takes a sponge and begins removing his make-up. "You see, I thought that being dead was holding me back. I looked at all those living, breathing clowns and I wanted their lives."

"Er, you took their lives?" says Klaus, sounding a little nervous that this investigation is about to take a turn for the worse.

Deadzo laughs. "Oh dear me, no. That's not what I meant. I wanted to be like them." He works the sponge around with his eyes closed. The make-up drips down his face in rivers of coloured goo. "I wanted to be alive."

"Ah." Klaus looks relieved.

"That's why I took the Monster Maker." He picks up a towel and rubs it on his face. As the towel falls away you see that his skin is no longer grey and rotting, but pink and raw. Deadzo is alive.

In one easy movement, he removes his red wig and reveals a head of short, spiky, bright purple hair.

"You used the Monster Maker to bring yourself back to life," says Klaus.

"I confess it was so," replies the miserable clown.

"So it was you who took the device from the doctor's house?"

"Oh no," says the clown. "I didn't even know about the wretched thing until I saw the goblins making off with it."

"You saw the goblins take it?"

"Yes, they were sneaking out with it. I had no idea what it was. So I asked the witches—"

"Bridget and Burnella Milkbird," says Klaus.

"Precisely. They told me what it was. I saw that as my chance so I followed the goblins home. I was planning to wait until they were out and steal it for myself but then I witnessed the young werewolf boy paying them a visit. When he left, he had the Monster Maker. He took it home. Once again, my plan was to get in and take the thing but I couldn't find the right moment. In my profession it's all about the right moment."

"When did that moment come?" says Klaus.

"Earlier this evening. He took it out and used it.

I've no idea what for but I snatched it once he'd finished with it."

"So you got what you wanted," says Klaus. "You're alive. You don't seem very happy about it."

"This is the tragedy," says the clown with a heavy sigh. "Tonight I discovered that the one thing I had going for me was the fact that I was dead. A real zombie clown has value. A man pretending to be a zombie clown is a joke … and not even a very funny one…" He holds up the roses and sobs.

"So where is the Monster Maker now?"

"Why, it's right here."

Deadzo pulls back the tablecloth and steps away. You peer under the table, expecting to see the Monster Maker, but it's not there.

"What are you trying to pull?" asks Klaus.

From the look on Deadzo's face, he's as confused as you. "But … I don't understand. It was there before my performance."

Your eyes shift to something else. Pushed to the side of the dressing table is a food wrapper with what looks like a half-eaten hot dog. Klaus follows your gaze and sees it too.

"Where did you get that?" he says.

"Those witches brought it in before the performance,"

says Deadzo. "It's the first thing I've had to eat since regaining my life. To be honest, it's not much tastier than brains."

Klaus turns to you and says what you're thinking. "The witches must have the Monster Maker."

You're already on your feet and out of the door, racing after your boss. You leave Deadzo behind and hurry out of the theatre into the street.

The witches' caravan is closed up with the awning pulled in. Their lumbering purple-haired monster is packing up the board and carrying it inside. Bridget spots you coming.

"Quick, get in!" she yells at the monster. "Get moving, Burnella!"

The monster steps into the caravan and the engine starts.

"Wait!" Klaus runs after the vehicle as it pulls away from the curb.

"Sorry," cries Bridget. "We've got another catering job to get to."

"Stop! Thieves!" cries Klaus. You're both pounding up the road in pursuit but the caravan has picked up speed so you stop chasing. You catch your breath, placing your hand on a bin, and notice something inside. You reach in and lift it out. It looks like a sewing machine covered in cogs. You inspect it closely and spot a few strands of purple hair. This is what you've been looking for. This is the object that can be used to create monsters or bring zombies back to life.

"What you got there, then?" asks Klaus.

You look up and smile.

He lifts the Monster Maker from your hands.

"I guess they had no further use for it." Klaus inspects it. "And so, if I've got this right, it was the goblins, the werewolf, the clown and, finally, the witches."

It's a lot to take in but you're pleased you've resolved the case and can finally return the stolen item.

"Good job." Klaus's words are as warm and welcome as a mug of hot chocolate. He's not one to overstate things or to overly enthuse, but it's all you need to hear. You performed your role. You did a good job. You found the Monster Maker. Maybe you don't understand everything that happened, but you've solved the mystery. The case is closed.

YOU HAVE REACHED ONE OF THE THREE POSSIBLE ENDINGS.

Turn to page 201
WHAT IF?

CONFRONTING FRANKLEFINK

KLAUS IS GNAWING ON THE sandwich you just handed him. You're feeling hungry as well, but you're too nervous to eat. You're standing outside Dr Franklefink's house, waiting for him to answer the door. You're worried because it was the doctor who hired you but your investigation has led you back to his doorstep. Are you really about to accuse your client of being the thief he's paying you to find?

Dr Franklefink opens the door.

"Oh, it's you," he says. "You'd better make it snappy. I'm going out soon."

You step into the hallway. You can see into the living room where the walls are lined with pictures of his ancestors, each standing proudly next to the monsters they made. The oldest ones are paintings and the more recent ones are photographs. You scan the walls, but the only picture of Monty you can see is a class photo on top of the fireplace.

"So, have you news about my Monster Maker?" Franklefink demands.

"I think we're getting closer, yes," says Klaus.

"But you haven't actually found it?" demands the doctor.

"Not yet," admits Klaus. "We have a few more questions to ask first."

"Questions?" snaps Dr Franklefink. "You've asked enough questions. All you've done is ask questions! What I need now is for you to prove that Bramwell Stoker took my Monster Maker, make the discovery public, then bring it back."

"Make it public?" Klaus considers the words as he repeats them. That was certainly an interesting thing to say.

"Yes. If Stoker thinks he can waltz in and steal from me he has another think coming."

"I imagine a vampire would be more inclined

151

to tango than waltz," says Klaus.

"Whatever dance he did," says Franklefink, "just do what I'm paying you to do and go after Stoker!"

Klaus exchanges a glance with you. "Remind me, *what* are you employing us to do?"

"I'm beginning to wonder," says Dr Franklefink. "Any detective worth his salt would have noticed the bat droppings at the scene of the crime and understood that there really was only one suspect: Bramwell Stoker."

Yetis are famously mild-mannered and you don't often see your boss get angry, but you know what it means when his fur bristles. Klaus is getting wound up.

"I have a problem with your poop proof," says Klaus. "Bramwell Stoker is a vampire, and one crime that rarely gets attributed to vampires is breaking and entering. Do you know why?"

"Why?" says Dr Franklefink.

"Vampires have to be *invited in* to houses," says Klaus. "Did you invite him in?"

The doctor adjusts a vase on a shelf, revealing a line of dust which he cleans with his finger. "I, er... Well, I've known him for some time. I dare say I have invited him in before."

"And another question that has been troubling

152

us," says Klaus. "If you suspected it was Stoker all along, why did you hire us?"

"You're the detective. You tell me," snarls Dr Franklefink.

"Do you know what I think?" Klaus walks into the living room, nudging the chandelier with his huge head. It jingles as it settles again. "I think this whole thing is a scam designed to drag Stoker's name through the mud. I wouldn't be surprised if the Monster Maker was hidden right here in the house."

"Utter rubbish," says Dr Franklefink. "I'm not paying you to accuse me."

"What's wrong?" says Klaus. "Are you worried we're getting too close to the truth?"

"I don't know what you're talking about." Franklefink looks increasingly agitated by the direction the conversation is taking.

"One solution to this mystery is that you made it look like it was stolen because you wanted to ruin Stoker's chance in the forthcoming election, creating a public scandal by calling him a thief."

"Stoker doesn't need any

help from me when it comes to losing elections."
Franklefink sniggers.

"Yes, but this year he's up against you, a human,"
says Klaus.

"A human with an established history of creating
monsters," replies Franklefink.

"One small monster," Klaus corrects him.

"It will be two once I have my machine back,"
says Dr Franklefink.

"Be that as it may, if there's one thing the Shady
Side community mistrust more than a hairless wonder
like Stoker, it's a human. I'm just putting it out there
that you could have decided to tip the scales in
your favour."

"Pure fantasy," says Dr Franklefink. "Now, I must
prepare for tonight's debate with that thief Stoker.
Do your job, Mr Solstaag. Find my Monster
Maker and show the world that the vampire
cannot be trusted."

Dr Franklefink ushers you out of
the door but, as you're leaving, you
spot something upstairs. Monty is
peering through the bannisters,
his purple mop-like hair
hanging over his face.

As you catch his eye, he scuttles away.

Outside, Klaus turns to you. "Sometimes it helps to confront the suspects with your theories ... even the more outlandish ones. It allows you to read their reactions. I still don't trust the professor, but I think that next we should check out what the goblins are up to. Unless you have any better ideas?"

You're still wondering about Monty. Did he look guilty or is he just fed up? And if he did look guilty, is that a good enough reason to speak to him next, or should you go with Klaus's idea of finding the goblins?

? You agree with Klaus that it's time to talk to the goblins.
Turn to page 118
CREEPY PETE'S PIZZERIA

? No. You feel sure that the doctor's monster son knows more than he's letting on.
Turn to page 156
MAYBE MONTY

MAYBE MONTY

"If we want to talk to Monty, it's going to be a whole lot easier without his dad being around," says Klaus. "Which means we'll have to wait until one of them leaves the house."

You're sitting in the car, outside Dr Franklefink's home. Waiting and watching is all part of the job. You don't mind, because it gives you time to think, review your notes and try to work out the solution to this puzzle.

Klaus notices you're shivering in the icy blast of the air conditioning and pulls out a flask of hot chocolate. You clasp your hands around the cup and enjoy the sweet smell and the steam rising before you take a sip. It's delicious. As Klaus always tells you, yetis make the best hot chocolate.

As the chocolatey warmth fills your body, you sink into your seat. Your eyelids feel heavy. The only sound is Klaus's breathing. You feel tiredness wash over you but as your hands relax, hot chocolate slops out of the cup and you're suddenly wide awake.

"Look, something's happening," says Klaus.

The front door of the house is open. Dr Franklefink is leaving.

"He must be going to the Night Mayor debate at the City Chamber," says Klaus. "Duck down. We don't want to be seen."

You lower yourself in your seat but it is easier for you than for your large hairy boss. Thankfully the doctor is preoccupied and doesn't notice your car.

The moment he's driven away, Klaus says, "Right. We're up. Watson, stay here. No running off or honking at bigger cars."

You leave the car and walk to the house. Klaus has to ring the doorbell five times before Monty appears.

"How's it going, Monty?" asks Klaus.

"It's going but I'm not growing," he replies miserably.

"Can we come in?" asks Klaus.

"I suppose," says Monty. "Dad's not in. It's just me. Have you found his stupid Monster Maker yet?"

"We're getting closer. We're pretty sure we know who took it."

"Oh ... right." Monty nervously fiddles with his stitches. "Who?"

"Who do *you* think?" Klaus enquires.

Monty squirms. "Er, maybe the witches? I heard that they're making a monster."

"Who did you hear that from, then?" enquires Klaus.

"Lana told me. She gets everywhere, that ghost."

"Interesting," says Klaus. "But whether or not the witches had a use for the Monster Maker, I don't think they were the ones who took it. *Were* they, Monty?"

"I told you, I don't know," replies Monty, but his denial is becoming less convincing every time.

"We're ready for the truth now," says Klaus.

"The truth," repeats Monty.

"Yes."

"But..." Monty drops to the ground, a mess of purple hair and tears. You instantly feel sorry for him. This isn't a master criminal. This is a young child and he's upset.

Your boss feels the same. He places an arm round Monty and hugs him. You're so used to Klaus's gruff ways, but this isn't the first time you've seen him show compassion. He may spend his days investigating the shadier side of the world, but beneath all that fur beats the heart of a yeti who cares.

You've sometimes been on the receiving end of a yeti hug, so you understand why Monty's eyes are watering when Klaus finally releases him. He wipes away his tears, then pulls a thread to tighten the stitches around his eyes.

"I just want what any boy wants," he says.

"A Monster Maker?" says Klaus.

"To grow up and to have a parent who cares," says Monty. "Sometimes I even feel jealous of Huey."

"Huey's a werewolf, Monty," says Klaus.

"Yes, but most of time he's just a kid, and he'll grow bigger like the rest of them. And at least his mum cares about him. I can't grow and Dad doesn't give a hoot about me. He's more interested in making stupid Enormelda."

"Is that why you took the Monster Maker? To stop him?"

"Yes. I don't want him to make a mother for me! I want him to *be* a father."

"So why did you do it on your own birthday?" asks Klaus.

"I suppose I thought he wouldn't know it was me, if there were lots of people in the house. I thought he'd blame the goblins," Monty replies. "I took it from the lab. I hid it in my bedroom. I was just trying to make a point. I was going to put it back."

"So why didn't you?"

"Because when I checked in my room, it was gone."

"You're saying that someone stole it from your room?" asks Klaus. "When?"

"I think someone must have seen me take it in during the game of hide-and-seek."

"Why didn't you tell us before?"

"I was scared that Dad would be angry."

"I'm sure he'll understand," says Klaus. "You just wanted his attention. It wasn't your fault." Klaus gives Monty a moment to consider what he just said, then, softly, he asks, "Who could have seen you? Who do you think took it?"

Monty shrugs. "Bobby said it was Huey when I spoke to him on the phone after the party, but I think Bobby was just trying to get him in trouble."

"You and Huey aren't exactly friends," says Klaus. "Why did you invite him to your party?"

"Dad said I had to. I think he just wants his mum's vote in this stupid election."

Klaus nods and strokes his chin thoughtfully. "Last question. Do you want me to retrieve the Monster Maker?"

Monty looks shattered and worn. "I don't know… My dad doesn't listen. I don't want a mother. I don't want him to become Night Mayor and have even less time for me. I want him to be a father."

The tears are falling again.

"Monty, Dr Franklefink is driven by ambition and

a passion for science but he's also your father and he loves you. I think you'd better talk to him."

"He's at the City Chamber," says Monty.

"I guess we could take you there," says Klaus.

Your boss turns to you.

Do you agree? Should you give Monty a lift to see his father? You haven't yet recovered the Monster Maker so perhaps you should turn your attention back to Huey Cry. Klaus is waiting to see what you want to do.

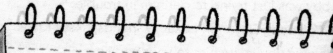

? Go and look for Huey.

Turn to page 163
SHEEPISH WOLF

? Take Monty to City Chamber.

Turn to page 170
CITY CHAMBER

SHEEPISH WOLF

ARRIVING AT THE CRYS' QUIET suburban home, you notice rose petals strewn all over the garden and scratch marks along the wooden fence.

Klaus steps out of the car and takes a deep breath. You see the swell of his mighty ribcage. He has the scent of something in his nostrils. Watson has smelled it too and is nervously revving his engine.

"Good boy," says Klaus, gently patting his bonnet. "There's nothing to worry about."

From the way your boss's fine white hairs are standing up, you can tell Klaus isn't as relaxed as he sounds.

"Let's check out the back garden," he says.

You follow him around the side of the building, noticing the neighbours' curtain twitch. You suspect it's not the first time they've observed unusual activity around the Cry household. There's a gate, which Klaus easily forces open. You pass pitchforks and wheelbarrows lined up along the side of the house, then you step into the back garden. At the bottom, under a willow tree, is a shed. There's a light on inside and you can hear movement from within.

You approach cautiously.

"Werewolves can be a bit ... unpredictable," says Klaus. "So ... er, just avoid... Well, try not to look too ... too edible."

He chuckles quietly, then leans in to listen at the door. You can hear muffled growls from inside but you can't make out any words. Klaus gently turns the door handle.

"Stay out!" barks Mrs Cry, preventing it from moving.

Klaus pushes harder and finally forces the door open.

You're not prepared for what lies inside. There, before your eyes, are two snarling, panting wolves. You can see no trace of their human selves and yet from their size and eyes, you recognize Huey Cry and his mother. This much you expected but, while Mrs Cry is covered in brown fur, Monty is bright purple.

"That's an interesting colour," says Klaus. "What did you do, Huey?"

"I'm sorry. I just wanted to fit in and look at me now-now-nooowl…" cries Huey.

"You don't have to say anything," interrupts his mother, with a protective growl at Klaus.

"It would be helpful if you did," says Klaus. "I can't work out what's happened here at all."

"I think it's obvious what's happening here. My son and I are in the middle of our monthly ritual."

"So I see," says Klaus, picking a chicken feather off the ground and inspecting it. "Been out, have you?"

"Yes, we stretched our legs and had a bite to eat and now we'll spend the rest of the evening here."

"Were you out together?" enquires Klaus.

"For the most part," replies Mrs Cry. "Huey left first, but I caught up with him."

"And discovered he'd turned purple?" asks Klaus, amused.

"It's probably just an age thing. Lots of werewolves change colour as they get older."

"They don't usually go purple," says Klaus. "Hm... I wonder..." he muses. "The Monster Maker creates hair that brings things to life, but Huey is already alive—"

"Worse luck," interrupts Huey. "If I was a zombie or a vampire, I wouldn't get picked on."

"Don't be silly, darling. Werewolves have been a part of the Shady Side community for as long as they have." It's strange that Mrs Cry's voice is so recognizable when it's coming from a wolf's jaws.

"Oh, I've got it." Klaus clicks his fingers. "You

thought you could use the Monster Maker to bring your inner wolf to life so you'd always be like you are now."

"Yes," admits Huey forlornly. "I just want to fit in at school."

"Did it work?" asks Klaus.

"We'll find out in the morning, won't we? But I hope for my son's sake that it did not," says Mrs Cry, glaring at Huey. "If you think life is difficult as a werewolf, imagine what it'll be like being permanently purple! You really didn't think this through, did you?"

"I... I... I didn't know I'd end up purple," says Huey. "I'll be the laughing stock of the pack." He walks in a small circle, then sits down with his tail thrown over his nose. "I'm so sorry, Mum."

"Oh, my darling cub." Mrs Cry strokes her son's head. "But I don't understand. You didn't have it when I picked you up."

"That's a good question," says Klaus. "How did you do it?"

Huey raises his tail and replies sheepishly. "I convinced the goblins to steal it for me. I let them win the game of hide-and-seek in exchange for them taking it home. I went to their place afterwards and took it from there."

"I see. So where is it now?" Klaus looks around.

"I don't know," admits Huey. "I didn't want to do it here in case Mum stopped me—"

"Which I would have," interrupts Mrs Cry.

"So I took it to the park earlier this evening and waited until it went dark. Then, after I'd used it, I kind of lost track of what happened," says Huey.

"It's often like that once we've turned," adds his mother.

"So you left it in the park?" asks Klaus.

"Yes, I think someone else was there. I was pretty wrapped up in what I was doing but I picked up a scent."

"What kind of scent?"

"I don't know. It smelled a bit funny ... and a bit like something that had died."

"Funny and dead," Klaus looks at you. "A zombie clown perhaps?"

"I think you've spent enough time interrogating my son," says Mrs Cry. "If it helps you find that wretched machine of Franklefink's, then I should also tell you that I noticed something purple around the witch's caravan while I was out tonight. Now, please leave."

"All right." Klaus walks to the door and opens it,

but pauses before leaving. "Thanks for being honest with us, Huey," he says. "Personally, I think it suits you."

"What? The purple hair?" replies Huey.

"The honesty," says Klaus, with a wry smile.

Seeing the look on Huey's face, you nudge Klaus and he adds, "And the hair, kid. You look great, you know. Special."

? Do you want to look for the witches next?

Turn to page 135

MILKBIRDS' MONSTER

? Or do you want to visit the theatre to see Deadzo?

Turn to page 183

THE MONSTER'S HAIR

CITY CHAMBER

KLAUS INSISTS ON GRABBING SOMETHING to eat on the way to City Chamber. He parks Watson outside a decidedly dodgy-looking kebab shop and offers to get something for you and Monty. Looking at the pictures of greasy kebabs, burgers and chips, you both decline. You can tell Monty is nervous from the way he keeps twiddling with his loose stitches.

While Klaus is getting his food, you wait in the car. Monty is in the back seat, and you sit in silence until he leans forwards and says, "Can you turn the radio on?"

There's no need for you to press the button. Watson is always listening. The radio comes on and you hear a presenter's voice.

"The debate is currently underway in City Chamber to decide who will be the next Night Mayor of Haventry. And with more on that story, let's go over to *News of the Unusual* reporter, Gretchen Barfly-Sewer."

"Good evening," replies a rasping female voice. "As we know, the Night Mayor is responsible for all the goings-on in the Shady Side of Haventry and these two contenders couldn't be offering more different visions of the future. As usual, Bramwell Stoker is looking to sink his teeth into the job, but this year, monster-making human Dr Franklefink has also thrown his hat into the ring."

"Great stuff, Gretchen," says the presenter. "And are things hotting up?"

"They are indeed," replies the reporter. "In fact, Dr Franklefink has just suggested that he's going to reveal information that he claims will prove decisive in this fiercely fought contest."

Klaus opens the door and drops into the driver's seat with a paper bag full of junk food.

"Right, let's go and resolve this thing," he says.

He eats while he drives, which would be dangerous if it weren't for the fact that Watson is perfectly capable of driving himself – even if that does occasionally involve stopping to sniff a lamp post.

"At the heart of every mystery there is one central question," says Klaus between mouthfuls. "But it's not always clear what that question is. Dr Franklefink wanted us to ask, *Who stole the Monster Maker?* But as we now know there was more than one person involved, the correct question is, *What happened to the Monster Maker?*"

"And what's the answer?" asks Monty.

"That's what we're about to find out," replies Klaus. "Look, we're here."

The City Chamber is in the heart of the Shady Side of Haventry. It's an old redbrick building with gargoyles on the side. Occasionally one of the gargoyles sneezes and the others glare at it angrily.

A bored-looking ogre at the door waves you all in.

The hall is packed. Members of the Shady Side community sit on rows of wooden chairs, panting, hissing, growling and snarling at Bramwell Stoker and Dr Franklefink.

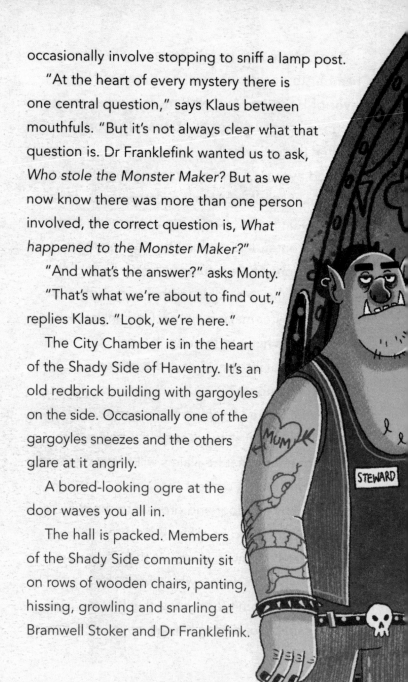

The two political rivals are mid-debate as they battle it out to become Haventry's next Night Mayor. Chief Inspector Darka, the minotaur chief of the Unusual Police Force, is sitting in the front row, arms folded, bullish eyes trained on the stage.

You spot Bobby Stoker in the audience. The goblins are there too. Lana the ghost is hovering above. There's no sign of the Crys, but since there's a full moon tonight, that's no surprise. The witches and Deadzo are absent too. You glance at Klaus, who's also scanning the room.

Both candidates have dressed up. Dr Franklefink is wearing a brand new lab coat, while Stoker is sporting a cape and top hat. They're sitting behind a large table with a dusty black cloth draped over it. In between them sits an elderly wizard with a beard down to his knees. He taps a large wooden staff on the table and cries, "Order, please. Show some decorum!"

No one listens until the wizard bangs his staff on the floor, sending a minor earthquake through the building and silencing everyone in the hall.

"Thank you." The wizard adjusts his glasses, which have slipped down his nose. "Now, Mr Stoker and Dr Franklefink, it's a simple question. What would you do about the problem of dragons gnawing through cables? Dr Franklefink."

"Thank you, Grand Master Dimbleby. The *bald* truth of the matter is—"

"Why, you insolent mortal!" Bramwell rises to his feet and snarls, revealing his yellow fangs.

"Please, keep this civil," says the wizard.

"Oh, we see his true colours now," says Dr Franklefink. "Once a vampire, always a vampire. Vote for me!"

"You?" spits Bramwell. "You have achieved nothing in your short life. You haven't even managed to produce a full-sized monster."

"And now he stoops to personal attacks," says Dr Franklefink.

"What do you call your remarks about my hairline?" says Bramwell. "Ladies and gentlemen, dead and undead, I hope you are seeing the true nature of my opponent. What do you want – a man who trades cheap jibes or a pillar of our community?"

"A pillar, eh?" Dr Franklefink turns to address the audience. "Good people of Haventry, I stand before you today bearing the shocking news that this man is a thief."

The crowd gasps in shock.

"Order, order." The wizard bangs his staff again, making a cloud of plaster dust fall from the ceiling. "Dr Franklefink, do you have anything to back up this accusation?"

"I do indeed." The doctor has noticed your boss. "This morning I hired a detective to solve this crime. Klaus Solstaag, please let everyone know what you have found out about this man."

Klaus makes his way to the front of the stage. He's in no hurry. He pauses, then turns to you. He beckons. "You too," he says. "And you, Monty."

Monty is reluctant. You feel the same, but you follow Klaus. Everyone's eyes are on you as you walk towards the stage. Monty is quivering. You steady your own hand too. You're still clutching your notebook.

"This is decidedly unconventional," says Grand Master Dimbleby.

"Yes, and my apologies," says Klaus. "But you see, I was hired by Dr Franklefink following the removal of the Monster Maker from his lab."

"It was a theft. And *he* stole it." Franklefink is pointing a finger at Bramwell. "There were bat droppings at the scene of the crime."

"Bat droppings that you placed there," interrupts Klaus.

"How dare you?" states Dr Franklefink.

"You called in the unicorn cleaning service to clear up the mess made by the goblins—"

"He poisoned my grand-gobbles with his nasty cake!" interrupts Ma Squelch from the audience.

Klaus nods. "But the point is that Uni-clean would have cleaned any actual evidence left by the thief, therefore the bat poop – if that's what it was – must have been placed there after they left."

"What?" cries the incensed doctor. "Outrageous!"

"Planting false evidence is outrageous, I agree," states Bramwell.

"Both of you, calm down." Grand Master Dimbleby waves his staff. Then he cries, "Silentium orator!" Both men are suddenly drawn back into their seats with their fingers on their lips, looking utterly bewildered and befuddled. The wizard smiles and says, "Now, Mr Solstaag, please continue. We must bring this matter to a conclusion so we can all move on. Did Bramwell steal the Monster Maker or not?"

"No, he did not." Klaus's words bring a hushed silence to the vast room.

"Then who in the blazes did?" demands Dimbleby.

"The thief – or should I say thieves – are in this hall."

Monty coughs. "Yes, I…" He hesitates – but

177

before he can continue, Bobby Stoker stands up and says, "I stole the Monster Maker."

The hall gasps. Bramwell Stoker glares at his son. "Sit down, Bobby!"

"Actually, I had the goblins steal it for me and then swore them to secrecy," says Bobby.

Grundle and Grinola stand up and speak in unison. "We don't know nothing about no Monster Maker."

"I told them to say that," says Bobby.

"Yeah, he did actually," admits Grundle.

"You stole it and didn't tell me?" asks Monty.

"Sorry, Monty," replies Bobby.

"But why?" asks Bramwell Stoker.

Bobby looks down, ashamed, and you notice that his hair is singed at the ends and that the follicles have a purple tinge. You grab Klaus's sleeve. He follows your gaze, then smiles at you.

"Nice work," he says, finally understanding Bobby's motive.

"The Monster Maker breathes life into the dead," says Klaus.

"As vampires, both you and your father are dead."

"It's been over two hundred years since I drew a breath," says Bramwell Stoker proudly.

"Yes, but your son hasn't been dead as long as you," says Klaus. "And the truth is you wish you weren't dead now, don't you, Bobby?"

Bobby fights back his tears but you can tell that Klaus's words hurt. He's hit the nail on the head.

"I don't understand," says Bramwell. "You come from a long line of vampires. I'm dead, your grandfather was dead. And his father before him."

"I'm sorry," sobs Bobby.

"Are you saying that this boy thought he could use my machine to bring himself to life?" asks Dr Franklefink.

"I tried," says Bobby. "I failed."

"But why?" Bramwell Stoker asks the question, but you can tell that everyone in the room is thinking it.

"I just want to be normal," admits Bobby. "I want to be human."

"Oh, my boy," cries Bramwell.

"Me too," says Monty.

"I-I never realized," Dr Franklefink replies.

You look around the room and wonder how many others feel the same. As one yourself, you could tell them that even when you are a human it doesn't necessarily mean you fit in, but this is not the moment to break your silence.

"Of course," says Klaus. "All that teasing poor Huey about being so ordinary most of the time, and the fact is you're jealous."

Bobby doesn't respond but, once again, you can tell that Klaus has got it right. If only Huey was here to witness this confession.

"So where is this machine now?" asks Grand Master Dimbleby, glancing at his watch.

"I have it." Bobby reaches down and picks up an object that's been hiding under his chair. When he holds it up, it looks like a sewing machine covered in copper cogs.

"My Monster Maker!" cries Dr Franklefink.

"Yes," says Klaus.

"I was going to return it," muttered Bobby. "I'm sorry I took it. It was stupid. It was selfish and it was..."

"Human," says Bramwell Stoker. "You see,

gathered folk of the Shady Side, we vampires may be dead but we still have hearts. even if they no longer pump our blood."

"I can't believe it..." says Dr Franklefink.

"What?" asks Bramwell.

"He's trying to use his son's thievery to garner sympathy. Could he stoop any lower?"

"Me?" says Bramwell. "I am the victim here."

"You? I was robbed by your son," proclaims Dr Franklefink.

"You planted false evidence!" yells Bramwell.

"Perhaps we could resume the debate," suggests Grand Master Dimbleby.

"Yes, I have a question about the drains," says a mermaid at the back of the room.

But other hands are shooting up and more residents are shouting about the problems and issues that affect them.

Klaus sticks out his hand to help you off the stage.

"Well done," he says. "There were a few twists at the end but we've found the Monster Maker and we've established who took it. I think we should get out of here before things get –" he pauses and glances around at the hall, which is buzzing with hissing outrage – "even uglier."

YOU HAVE REACHED ONE OF THE THREE POSSIBLE ENDINGS.

Turn to page 201
WHAT IF?

THE MONSTER'S HAIR

YOU'RE STANDING OUTSIDE BROCKLEY JACKS theatre, where Deadzo was performing tonight. You're here to question the zombie clown about his involvement with the theft of the Monster Maker, but the witches' caravan is parked outside. They've been serving food and drink to the crowd that just left the theatre.

"I had no idea a zombie clown was even capable of dying on stage," says one of the last customers to pick up a steaming cup of witches' broth.

Once the rush has died down, the exhausted witches sit slumped in deckchairs in front of the caravan. Their monstrous creation is sweeping up dropped food and bits of rubbish. He looks as dishevelled as them and the shower cap on his head has slipped back to reveal a shock of purple hair.

Klaus turns to you. "I know we're here for the clown, but I think we may have a new line of enquiry."

It's clear that the witches have used the Monster Maker to bring their creation to life. The hair is a complete giveaway. Whatever your suspicions were about Deadzo, you need to talk to the witches first.

"Approach carefully," warns Klaus. "One thing I've learned doing this job is that it's best to act with caution around anyone who has the power to turn you into something else. I wasn't always a yeti, you know." He laughs. "I'm joking," he explains. "I've always been a yeti but the point still stands. Be careful."

You keep one step behind him, mindful of his warning.

"Busy night?" Klaus asks the witches.

"Yes, very busy, and we're having a much-needed rest," says Burnella.

As far you can tell, it's the purple-haired monster who's doing most of the work.

"I think I get what's happened," says Klaus, looking down at the resting witches. "You stole the Monster Maker so you could create a servant to do your work while you loll about."

"How dare you?" says Bridget. "We're not lolling. I've never lolled in my life. And we are hard-working, honest witches."

Burnella emits a high-pitched cackle. "We're as honest as the night is long."

"Oh, it has been a long night," says Bridget. "Hey, Boris, get me another steaming broth on the rocks, would you?"

"Broothhhh," moans the monster. "Rocksssss."

"I told you. We are not calling him Boris," says Burnella.

"Boris was my grandfather's name."

"We're sisters, and no it wasn't. Boris was the name

185

of that wizard you ran off to Casablanca with in 1936."

"Oh yes, a lovely young man," says Bridget wistfully. "What happened to him?"

"I think you turned him into a pelican in the end, didn't you?"

"That's right. We had a lovely dinner and then he ended up with an enormous bill." She cackles. "Do you get it? Enormous bill."

"I don't think turning people into things is a laughing matter," says Klaus.

"No sense of humour, yetis." Bridget tuts.

"What do you want, Klaus?" says Burnella.

"We came here to speak to Deadzo but the hair on your monster's head is a dead giveaway that you used the Monster Maker to bring him to life."

"I told you to dye his hair," says Burnella.

"You did not," replies Bridget.

"Well, I meant to," admits Burnella.

Klaus nudges you. You've found your culprits, but not everything is crystal clear yet.

"Why use the Monster Maker when you could use your own magic to bring Boris – or whatever his name is – to life?" asks Klaus.

"Do you know how hard it is bringing things to

life?" squawks Bridget.

"Can't say I do," says Klaus.

"Well, it's very hard," says Bridget. "One of the hardest spells for a witch to perform. You have to recite pages of incantations, your arms get exhausted from all that waving, and don't even get me started on the stirring. Ooh, the stirring."

"She's right," says Burnella. "Much easier to use the Monster Maker."

"Where is it now?" asks Klaus, glancing at the open caravan door.

The monster steps in the way of it. You look into his sunken eyes and wonder how much he understands. For all his massive bulk, in terms of age he's a new-born baby.

"Nooooo gooooo," he moans.

"Good lad, Boris," says Bridget.

"Booorrrisssss," repeats the monster.

"We are not calling him Boris," snaps Burnella, before turning back to Klaus. "Now, hop off before I turn you into a frog."

"A frog?" says Bridget. "Honestly, you have no imagination. Why not turn him into something interesting like a two-toed sloth?"

"I don't know the spell for that," admits Burnella.

"That's a relief. Now, hand over the Monster Maker," demands Klaus.

"We could do that," says Burnella. "Or you could go and talk to the clown first. Aren't you interested to know how he fits into all this?"

She's addressing Klaus but somehow her eyes are also focused on you. You feel sure that the Monster Maker is in the caravan but you wonder if she has a point. Was Deadzo involved? Or is she using magical powers of persuasion to send you off in the wrong direction?

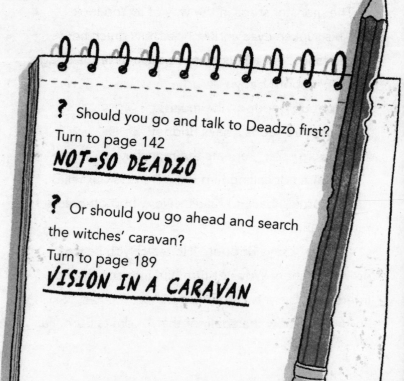

? Should you go and talk to Deadzo first?

Turn to page 142

NOT-SO DEADZO

? Or should you go ahead and search the witches' caravan?

Turn to page 189

VISION IN A CARAVAN

VISION IN A CARAVAN

THE PURPLE-HEADED MONSTER BLOCKS THE door to the caravan, his huge arms folded in a way that looks uncomfortable.

"Step aside, Boris," says Klaus.

"I told you, we're not calling him Boris," says Burnella.

"Basil?" suggests Bridget.

"Why do they all have to begin with B?" asks Burnella.

"All my boyfriends' names started with B, now I think about it," replies Bridget.

"Half of your boyfriends *ended up* as bees," says Burnella, cackling with laughter.

"How about Brian?" says Bridget. "He looks like a Brian."

The caravan rattles irritably. "Nope. Susan doesn't like that one," says Burnella.

"Bootsy?" suggests Bridget.

"Oh, I like that one. Let's call him Bootsy," says Burnella.

"Boooootsy," echoes the monster.

"Oh, I've had enough of this." Klaus pushes past the monster and steps inside. "Keep your guard up," he says to you. "This caravan used to be a witch so the magic inside can be pretty pungent. Things might get a bit weird."

You try not to show your fear as you follow your boss inside. Klaus was right to warn you. It's like stepping into someone else's dream. There are stars beneath your feet. Grass grows above your head. You feel as small as an insect and as large as a mountain. Your stomach lurches, as though you're standing on a precipice, trying not to fall. You jump. You fly and you land. If Klaus is still near you, he's shrouded by the magic that fills your head.

You blink.

You're no longer in the caravan. You're standing in the centre of Dr Franklefink's lab, looking at a sewing machine covered in cogs, with purple thread hanging from a needle. The Monster Maker.

The door opens and Monty steps into the room. He walks straight through you as though you're not there. It's a disconcerting sensation. You feel like a ghost. You consider the possibility that you are, but no, you're alive; this is a vision of the past.

You can hear Huey calling, "Coming! Ready or not!" Monty looks around furtively then picks up the machine and carries it out of the lab.

"Monty took it." Klaus's voice speaks the words somewhere near you. You cannot see him but he must be watching the same thing.

The scene shifts and suddenly you're standing in Monty's bedroom, once again with the Monster Maker.

"Let's hide in here," says Grundle, entering the room.

"We usually just hide behind each other," says Grinola.

"OK. Let's do that in here," says Grundle.

They step into the room and Grinola walks straight into the Monster Maker. "Ow," she complains, grabbing her foot with both hands and toppling over.

"Ha!" says Huey Cry, bursting into the room.

Grundle and Grinola quickly try to hide behind each other, until they walk backwards into a cabinet, causing a basketball to fall off the top and somehow land on both their heads. It's pretty funny but Huey is more interested in the device.

"Er. Have you found us, Huey?" enquires Grundle.

"I don't *have to* have found you," replies Huey.

"What's that mean?" says Grinola.

"I mean, if you do me a favour I could promise not to find you until the end of the game. What do you think?"

The goblin twins look at each other.

"We've never won at hide-and-seek before," says Grundle.

"We've never won at nothing," adds Grinola.

"We'll do it," they both say, speaking in unison.

"Great. So all you have to do is wrap up this big machine thing and sneak it out when you leave. I'll come round to your place later and pick it up."

"Why? Is it yours?" asks Grundle.

"Yes, of course," lies Huey. "But don't tell anyone about it. OK? Goblins' honour."

"Goblins' honour," says Grundle.

"I ain't never heard of goblins' honour," says Grinola.

"Never mind," says Huey. "Now, I'll go and find the others. You hide in the party room."

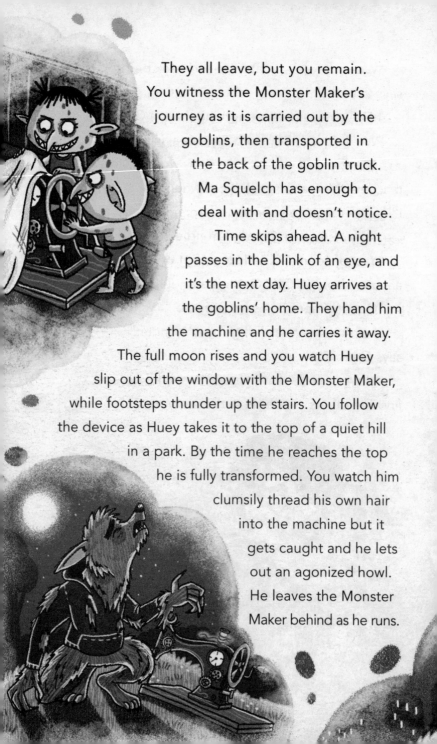

They all leave, but you remain.
You witness the Monster Maker's
journey as it is carried out by the
goblins, then transported in
the back of the goblin truck.
Ma Squelch has enough to
deal with and doesn't notice.
Time skips ahead. A night
passes in the blink of an eye, and
it's the next day. Huey arrives at
the goblins' home. They hand him
the machine and he carries it away.
The full moon rises and you watch Huey
slip out of the window with the Monster Maker,
while footsteps thunder up the stairs. You follow
the device as Huey takes it to the top of a quiet hill
in a park. By the time he reaches the top
he is fully transformed. You watch him
clumsily thread his own hair
into the machine but it
gets caught and he lets
out an agonized howl.
He leaves the Monster
Maker behind as he runs.

You understand that Huey was trying to use the machine to bring to life his inner wolf, in the hope that it would make him fit in at school. The magic inside the caravan makes your head spin.

But the vision has already moved on from Huey. The Monster Maker is on the move again.

Lurking in the darkness, two dead eyes were watching. A pair of red gloves picks the machine up. Deadzo the zombie clown has followed Huey here and now he staggers down the hill, through the streets and into his dressing room.

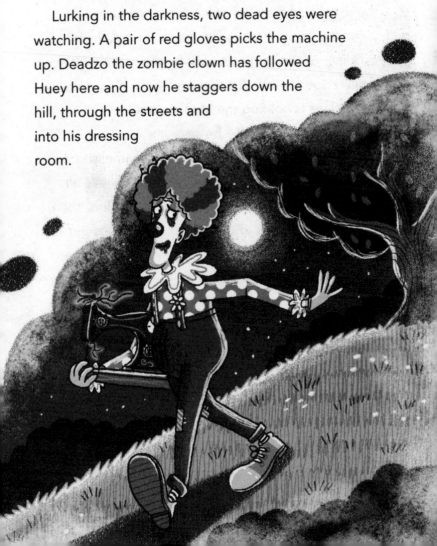

Deadzo switches on the machine, with tears streaming down his blotchy face.

"Dead no more," he mutters. "Let's see them turn me down for auditions now I'm alive again."

You think it must finally be the end of the Monster Maker's journey, but a bell rings and Deadzo leaves the room to the sound of lacklustre applause.

As the image melts away, you hear a pair of cackling voices. You turn and, for the first time since you stepped inside the caravan, you see your boss's face. Klaus is holding the Monster Maker.

"Look what I found," he says.

You're wondering if your boss just witnessed the same vision when he says, "If we're to believe all that, it was stolen by Monty, then the goblins, then Huey, then Deadzo. But how did the witches get hold of it? We know they used it to bring their monster to life and I think that vision cut out just as we were about to witness them enter the dressing room."

You step outside but the witches and the monster are no longer there. You hear an engine rev and the caravan pulls away.

"See you!" yells Bridget.

"Wouldn't want to be you!" adds Burnella. Both are sitting up front.

"Be yooooouuu," moans the monster.

"Hey!" cries Klaus, but Burnella is gripping the steering wheel and has her foot on the accelerator.

"Those witches are so tricksy," says Klaus. "But we have the device. I think we can return it and call the case closed. And it seems that Franklefink was wrong about Bramwell Stoker. According to that vision, he was one of the few suspects *not* involved."

Your boss hands the Monster Maker to you and says, "You did good."

Klaus is never one to overly praise but you understand from these few words that he's pleased with the job you've done. He may have been leading the investigation, asking all the questions, but you reached this conclusion and solved the case because of the decisions you made. You smile to yourself.

"I think we'd better take this back to the doctor," says Klaus.

———————————————

YOU HAVE REACHED
ONE OF THE THREE
POSSIBLE ENDINGS.

Turn to page 201
WHAT IF?

WHAT IF?

YOU'RE BACK IN THE FREEZING-COLD office, exhausted but relieved that you've done your job and solved the mystery. You open a drawer and place your notebook inside. You pull the pencil from your pocket and notice a single purple hair is wrapped around it. You unwind the hair and hold it between your fingers, pulling it taut.

"What have you got there?" asks Klaus. He's settled behind his desk with two fans blowing directly at his huge hairy feet, wiggling his toes and enjoying the refreshing breeze.

You hold up the purple hair and show him.

"I can tell what you're thinking," he says. "It's common enough after a Shady Side investigation. You're still wondering *what if*?"

As he speaks, you continue to examine the strand of hair between your fingers, careful not to let it blow away.

"What if we'd followed this suspect rather than that one?" says Klaus. "What if our investigation had led us in a different direction? What did we miss?"

As he asks these questions, the hair between your fingers begins to glow. At first you think you're imagining it but the tighter you pull it, the brighter it becomes. You've spent all this time searching for the Monster Maker, but only now does it occur to you what a remarkable object it is.

There was a time, not long ago, when the idea of such a machine would have been laughable to you. Before you answered the job advert in that strange newspaper you would have dismissed it as fantasy. But those days are behind you. Your eyes have been opened. You've seen so much more of the world than you ever dreamed possible. Life on the Shady Side of Haventry has revealed a new normal.

"Hey, are you even listening?" asks Klaus.

You realize you'd drifted off. Something about this strand of hair between your fingers has infected your thoughts. You wonder if it can bring the past to life. Could you go back and solve this mystery again? What would you discover if you did things differently? Which point would you go back to? All the way to the beginning ... or to a moment when you could have gone in a different direction?

"The truth is a slippery thing." Klaus gets up and lifts a hat from the stand next to the door. "Watch," he says.

He throws the hat. It flies across the room and hits the stand but slides straight off and lands on the ground. He walks across the office, picks it up, returns to the desk and throws it again. This time it lands perfectly on the hat stand.

"Same throw," says Klaus. "Same hat. Different result. Hard to explain, isn't it? My advice is, don't waste too much time worrying about it. Enjoy it when the hat lands on the stand and don't dwell on the times it doesn't."

You understand he isn't just talking about hats. You wrap the purple hair around your finger. It sparkles and glows. There is magic in this strand and somehow you understand that this doesn't have to be the end. You can go back. You can discover more. You can even reach a different conclusion. But should you?

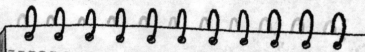

? Do you want to go back to the beginning?

Turn to page 11

THE MISSING MONSTER MAKER

? Or would you rather go back to the school pick-up?

Turn to page 93

HOME TIME

? Or if you want to call it a day and move
on to the next case, pick up a copy of

SOLVE YOUR OWN MYSTERY: THE TIME THIEF

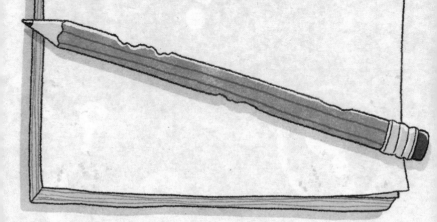

Name: Dr Frank F. Franklefink

Species: Human

Age: 52

Hobbies/Interests: Science, (re)animation and local politics

Most likely to say:

"Could you lend me a hand? Also, a kneecap if you have one."

"It's alive! Yes! Alive... Oh no. What have I done?"

Name: Montague "Monty" Franklefink

Species: Monster (but made of mostly human parts)

Age: 9

Hobbies/Interests: Playing hide-and-seek, riding his bike and sewing (up his own stitches)

Most likely to say:

"Apparently, I've got my grandad's eyes ... and my second cousin's little toe."

"I asked Dad if he would make me a foot taller, but he said he didn't have any more feet to spare."

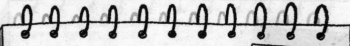

Name: Huey Cry

Species: Werewolf

Age: 11

Hobbies/Interests: Eating chicken, playing tag and chasing chickens

Most likely to say:

"No, I have no idea why there are chicken feathers all over the garden."

"I had a bad night but I'm all right noooooooow."

Name: Trisha Cry

Species: Werewolf

Age: 43

Hobbies/Interests: Butchery, hunting and embroidery

Most likely to say:

"No, my son has nothing to do with those chicken feathers all over the garden."

"Would you care for a chicken drumstick?"

Name: Ma Squelch

Species: Goblin

Age: 763 in goblin years (76 in human years)

Hobbies/Interests: Wrestling, mischief-making and knitting

Most likely to say:

"No, officer, my grand-gobbles never glued no dog to no wall!"

"What do you mean, Grinola's hand is still stuck to the dog?"

Names: Grundle and Grinola Squelch

Species: Goblin

Age: 84 in goblin years (8½ in human years)

Hobbies/Interests: Causing trouble, playing with animals and using glue sticks

Most likely to say:

"That's not what I meant when I said we should go play stick with the dog."

"Grinola, stop patting the dog! You've still got glue on your… Oh, never mind."

Name: Bramwell Stoker

Species: Vampire

Age: 256

Hobbies/Interests: Blood, bats and local politics

Most likely to say:

"Sorry, I can't eat that. I have a garlic intolerance."

"Oh yes, I'd love an invitation to come round for a nibble."

Name: Bobby Stoker

Species: Vampire

Age: 11 (although he's been 11 for a long time now)

Hobbies/Interests: Bobby enjoys any game involving a bat but mostly he likes just hanging around

Most likely to say:

"I'm not getting in a flap, Dad."

"No, I don't have a cold. It's just a little coffin."

Names: Burnella and Bridget Milkbird

Species: Witch

Ages: No one dares ask

Hobbies/Interests: Potion brewing, spell-making and catering

Most likely to say:

"You remind me of a cat I once owned. Yes, you look very familiar."

"You remind me of a warlock I once dated. Yes, you look just like my hex-boyfriend."

Name: Deadzo the Dead (Funny) Clown

Species: Zombie

Age: 42 when he died 107 years ago

Hobbies/Interests: Juggling, tumbling and eating brains

Most likely to say:

"I just ate a clown friend of mine, but he tasted a bit funny."

"Seriously? Has no one around here got any brains?"

Name: Lana MacCabe

Species: Ghost

Age: 9, although she was born in 1845

Hobbies/Interests: Grave dodging and hanging out in the usual haunts

Most likely to say:

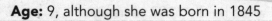

"Sometimes I feel as though you can't even see me."

"Don't mind me. I'm just passing through."

ABOUT THE AUTHOR

GARETH P. JONES
is the Blue Peter
Award-winning author
of over forty books
for children of all
ages, including
*The Thornthwaite
Inheritance, The Considine Curse* and *Death
or Ice Cream*. His series fiction includes Ninja
Meerkats, Adventures of the Steampunk Pirates,
Pet Defenders and Dragon Detective.

Gareth regularly visits schools all over the
world as well as performing at festivals.
He plays ukulele, trumpet, guitar, accordion
and piano to varying levels of incompetence.
He lives in south-east London with his wife
and two children.

ABOUT THE ILLUSTRATOR

LOUISE FORSHAW
is an illustrator from
the north east, living
just outside Newcastle
upon Tyne.

She lives with her
fiancé and three noisy
Jack Russell Terriers:
Lilah, Piper and Bandit.

To date, Louise has illustrated over
fifty children's books. When she isn't
drawing yeti detectives or being
barked at by her dogs, she loves
reading lots of books and binge-
watching TV shows about
vampires.